THE OTHER HALF OF LIFE

A NOVEL BASED ON THE TRUE STORY
OF THE MS *ST. LOUIS*

Kim Ablon Whitney

D0964834

Copyright © 2009 by Kim Ablon Whitney

All rights reserved. Published in the United States by Laurel-Leaf, an imprint of Random House Children's Books, a division of Random House, Inc., New York. Originally published in hardcover in the United States by Alfred A. Knopf, an imprint of Random House Children's Books, a division of Random House, Inc., New York, in 2009.

Laurel-Leaf Books with the colophon is a registered trademark of Random House, Inc.

Visit us on the Web! www.randomhouse.com/teens

Educators and librarians, for a variety of teaching tools, visit us at
www.randomhouse.com/teachers

The Library of Congress has cataloged the hardcover edition of this work as follows:
Whitney, Kim Ablon.
The other half of life : a novel based on the true story of the MS St. Louis / Kim Ablon Whitney.
p. cm.
Includes bibliographical references.
Summary: In 1939, fifteen-year-old Thomas sails on a German ship bound for Cuba with more than nine hundred German Jews expecting to be granted safe haven in Cuba.
ISBN 978-0-375-85219-0 (trade) — ISBN 978-0-375-95219-7 (lib. bdg.) —
ISBN 978-0-375-85355-5 (e-book)
1. Jews—Germany—History—1933–1945—Juvenile fiction. 2. Holocaust, Jewish (1939–1945)—Juvenile fiction. [1. Jews—Germany—History—1933–1945—Fiction. 2. Holocaust, Jewish (1939–1945)—Juvenile fiction. 3. Refugees, Jewish—Fiction. 4. Ships—Fiction.] I. Title.
PZ7.W61547Ot 2009
[Fic]—dc22
2008038949

ISBN 978-0-375-84422-5 (pbk.)

RL: 6.2

Printed in the United States of America
Map by Joe LeMonnier

10 9 8 7 6 5 4 3 2 1

First Laurel-Leaf Edition

For Cam and Luke

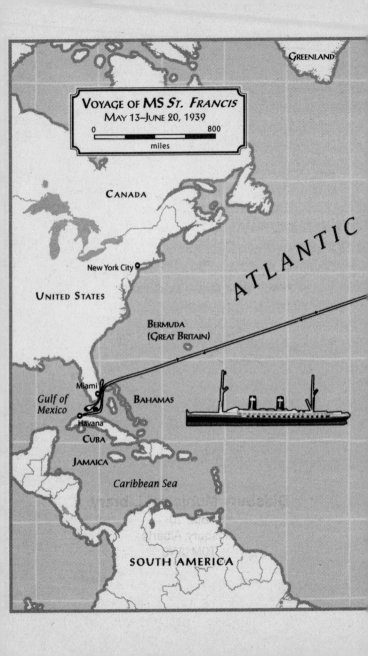

VOYAGE OF MS *ST. FRANCIS*
MAY 13–JUNE 20, 1939

0   800
miles

GREENLAND

CANADA

New York City

UNITED STATES

BERMUDA
(GREAT BRITAIN)

ATLANTIC

Miami

Gulf of Mexico

BAHAMAS

Havana

CUBA

JAMAICA

Caribbean Sea

SOUTH AMERICA

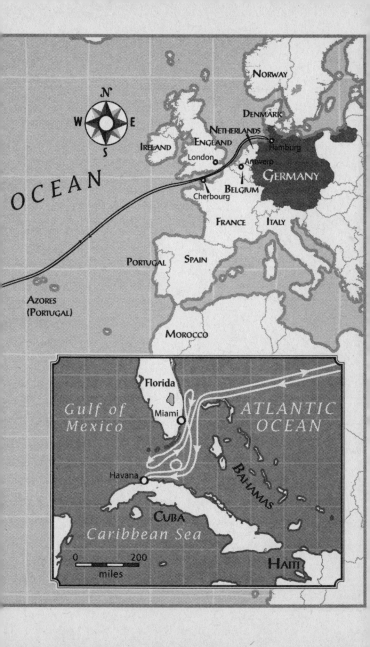

Chapter One

At the shed in Hamburg his mother took him by both shoulders. They had traveled hours on the train from Berlin, and she would be making the return trip without him. Since arriving, they had passed an uncomfortable hour rarely talking as they waited for boarding to begin. Finally it was time. The strong sea air surrounded them, making Thomas's tweed jacket feel heavy and damp. He noticed a sheen of moisture on his mother's cheeks and forced himself to focus on her eyes. In the past year, since his father was taken away by the Nazis, Thomas had always tried to look mostly at his mother's eyes. If he concentrated on her eyes, he could ignore the gauntness of her face, how he could picture her bony skull right there beneath her skin.

"I'm not going to cry and you're not either," she said, straightening his tie. Usually Thomas would have been annoyed at his mother's fussing, but he knew this might be the last time they would be together, at least for a long time.

She turned away, to face the ship. It had a giant black hull with rows of portholes above it. The way it sat so high in the water was impressive. The pedal boats Thomas was familiar with from a handful of days spent at the Wannsee were so small you could trail your hand in the water without even leaning over far. But on this great ship even the first deck loomed hundreds of feet above the surface of the water. Thomas's stomach felt queasy but he tried to ignore it.

His mother kept looking at the ship, and Thomas wondered if she was thinking whether there might be a way she could steal aboard. At six hundred reichsmarks, even securing one ticket to Cuba had been a miracle. Thomas had not known his parents had that much money hidden away. His mother had told him that they had been saving it for a time just like this—a chance to get out. Perhaps they had once hoped it would be enough for all three of them to escape Germany, but with the extra fees and dues tacked on by the German travel agency and the Reich, not to mention the price of the ticket from the shipping line itself, the money had barely covered Thomas's passage.

Neither Thomas nor his mother was foolish enough to think Thomas's father would ever come home; yet leaving Germany altogether seemed like betraying him, like giving up. Which was why even if they had been able to scrounge up enough money for two tourist fares, his mother still would not have gone.

It was also why Thomas himself didn't want to go.

"No tears," his mother repeated.

"You think I'd cry?" Thomas said. He had been strong through everything that had happened to them; he wasn't about to cry now.

"I'm not going to wait while you board," she continued as if she hadn't heard him. "I'm going to turn around and you're not going to look back. This is the right thing to do—the only thing to do."

Thomas fingered the ivory pawn in his pocket. He'd taken it from his father's chess set before leaving. "This isn't what Vati would have wanted. He would have wanted me to stay—"

She cut him off. "And look out for me?"

"No, he would have wanted me to stay and fight." He knew his mother didn't need him—a *Mischling,* half-breed. He would only be trouble to her. She was better off without him, as she was without his father. Without them she was of pure kindred blood, with the light hair and blue eyes to prove it.

His mother lowered her head. "There is no more fighting. Only surviving."

She pulled him to her. Thomas stiffened and then softened. At fifteen he felt too old for embraces, but the pressure of her body reminded him that he had not gotten to feel his father's arms around him a last time. He held tight, not wanting to let go. She smelled faintly of their apartment, the deep, musky scent of well-worn leather furniture. Thomas used to love how when he stood up from the sofa, his impression always remained on the seat cushion, as if the sofa were waiting for his return. Only now he would never be back.

Herr Kleist, who had been waiting nearby, stepped forward. "I'll watch out for him, you needn't worry, Frau Werkmann."

Herr Kleist was nearing seventy and one of his eyes constantly watered. He was a great-uncle of a friend of a friend. Thomas didn't have much faith in him. Also, he didn't need a guardian.

All around them, others bid tearful good-byes to family and friends. Porters in uniforms and caps scurried by with baggage. German mixed with Polish, Russian, and Yiddish.

Herr Kleist cleared his gravelly throat. "We should move on. They need to get the tourist class on before first class can board and we can set off."

Thomas stepped away from his mother. She had said no tears but he could hear her muffling sobs in her sleeve. He inhaled the salty air as gulls screeched overhead. He looked up at the two giant funnels and the mast of the ship. A swastika flag flapped in the breeze. Why hadn't he noticed it before? Thomas shivered in his damp clothes. How could a ship that was supposed to carry its passengers to freedom bear the Nazi flag?

Halfway up the sloping gangway, Thomas felt the intense desire to turn around, to see his mother one more time, to see whether she'd lived up to her promise of leaving after she'd failed at not crying. But he was afraid too. He didn't want to see his mother as he'd last seen his father: weakened and powerless.

A family of four walked abreast in front of them. The mother and daughter were dressed in long skirts with kerchiefs over their hair. The father and the older son wore black suits and hats. "At least we'll make it on before sunset," the man said to his wife.

Beside Thomas, Herr Kleist slouched along, shoulders bowed, head down, as if he hadn't paid his fare and was trying to slip on unnoticed. Thomas stretched himself taller and announced his arrival with solid footsteps that rattled the slats of the gangway.

They stepped aboard the ship and a steward met them, hands outstretched to relieve Herr Kleist of his worn leather suitcase.

Herr Kleist pulled back, clutching the case to his frail body. Thomas felt sorry for him—if the steward really intended to take away his case, or do anything else to Herr Kleist for that matter, Herr Kleist would be helpless to stop him.

"It's already been searched at Customs," Thomas blurted out to the steward. "What more do you want?" The search had been more than thorough, with the officials emptying people's pockets to make sure they hadn't brought more than the ten reichsmarks allowed them. Some had tried to smuggle jewelry or china on board, but it had been promptly confiscated. Out of spite, Thomas had almost felt like handing over his ten reichsmarks—it was so little money it was practically worthless. All it might buy would be a single meal in Cuba.

Herr Kleist shot Thomas a look of warning, his eyes narrow. He told the steward, "By all means, search my case. It's only what's allowed—nothing more."

"No need to look," the steward said, smiling. "I just wanted to offer to help carry it to your cabin."

Thomas surveyed the steward: the shiny gold buttons of his uniform, his fair skin, his light hair. He was young and handsome, with a nice smile. His good looks irked Thomas. He wished he were ugly so it would be even easier to detest him. Around his arm he wore the Nazi Party badge: a black swastika with a red circle around it. Thomas found his eyes drawn to the swastika even though just the sight of it was enough to give him chills. The Party badge confirmed what Thomas already knew—that all the people running the ship would be Nazis. Thomas had asked his mother again and again: "Why are they letting us go on a luxury liner?" It didn't make sense to him: The Nazis despised the Jews, so why let a whole ship of them travel on the same luxury liner that affluent people took on holidays?

"They want us out," his mother had answered. "Any way they can."

But it still didn't add up in Thomas's mind, and he planned to find out more once on board. It was like a new chess opening his father taught him—no matter how many times his father explained the moves, he couldn't fully understand until he had played it himself.

"If you show me your boarding card, I can direct you to your cabin," the steward offered.

"We have boarding cards, if that's what you're after," Thomas said. "We're not trying to steal aboard."

"Boy!" Herr Kleist warned Thomas. He took out his card and held it out to the steward. "Here we are. *Alles ist in Ordnung.*" Herr Kleist looked sharply at Thomas and snapped, "Your card!"

Thomas took out his boarding pass and with it his immigration identification card issued by the Cuban government. Most of the text was in Spanish. The only words Thomas could understand were: THOMAS WERKMANN, MS ST. FRANCIS, HAMBURG, GERMANY, MAY 13, 1939. The identification card also had a big red "J" on it that Thomas tried to overlook.

The steward glanced at their papers. "D Deck, right this way."

As they followed the steward down to the lower level of the ship, he told them that dinner would be served at seven in the tourist-class dining room. Thomas watched Herr

Kleist straighten slightly as the steward spoke. This was not the way the Nazis spoke to Jews. They usually only ordered and insulted. Thomas couldn't understand why the steward was showing them such respect—they weren't even first-class passengers. It was one thing to let them travel on a luxury liner, but it was another thing altogether to treat them well. He could sense Herr Kleist settling into this new order of things, but Thomas could not believe the treatment would last.

The passageway to the cabins seemed like any other hallway except for the low ceiling and the handrails, which Thomas realized must be in case of stormy seas. The steward opened the cabin door and held out his hand. "Here we are."

The cabin was plainly furnished with four wooden bunks, a washbasin, and a shaving mirror. The steward asked Herr Kleist if there was anything else he could do for him.

"No thank you," Herr Kleist replied.

"Have a pleasant voyage," he said.

"Did you hear that?" Herr Kleist said to Thomas as the steward left. "He wished me a pleasant voyage." Herr Kleist moved to one of the lower bunks and fingered the sheets. "And look at these: clean and starched." He let out a satisfied sound, as if a long journey were ending, not beginning.

Thomas walked to the porthole. He tried the handle but

it was locked tight. Thomas figured this low on the ship, he'd better get accustomed to the stale air.

Herr Kleist turned to Thomas, his face solemn again. He wagged his finger at him. "You will not be putting me in danger with your sharp tongue. Do you know what I've lived through? Have you had to scrub the streets with a toothbrush?"

Thomas thought about telling Herr Kleist what he *had* lived through. Something, in his opinion, much worse than scrubbing streets.

"I've gotten you aboard," Herr Kleist added. "Now you're on your own."

Thomas thought of his mother—how Herr Kleist had promised her he'd watch out for him. But promises meant nothing these days. Thomas didn't answer. He walked away. Alone was just fine with him.

Chapter Two

The first thing Thomas wanted to see was the upper deck. It took him a while to find his way through the ship's maze of rooms, passages, and stairwells. He walked by the gymnasium, the nursery, the beauty salon, and the shipboard store. It was like a regular town, only on the water. He peered in the windows of the store at the arrangements of postcards, cigars, toys, and clothing. A woman was touching the fabric of a dress and Thomas heard her ask the clerk, "Where is this wool from? It seems heavy for worsted wool." She soon introduced herself to the clerk, her chin held high: "My name is Blanka Rosen. I used to have the premier design shop in all of Prague." Thomas shook his head and kept walking. All of them used to be something else. All of them used to have more than they had now—a home, a family, a profession, a life. But none of it mattered anymore, and Thomas didn't see why people insisted on clinging to the past. Memories of what used to be only brought more pain.

Thomas had just set foot on the deck when a man in uniform stepped in front of him.

"Erste Klasse?"

"Macht es einen Unterschied?" Thomas asked.

The man stood at least a foot over Thomas. He had a big head too, with what Thomas noticed were strangely small ears, as if they had been forgotten at birth and carelessly put on later. He wore a different uniform than the steward who had shown them to the cabin. His uniform was the green jacket, green trousers, and black boots of a Nazi officer. Thomas wondered if he was an officer of the ship or of the Nazi Party.

"The upper deck is only for first-class passengers."

Thomas felt the sting of insult just the same way he had when he had been turned away at school for being a Jew. On that day he had arrived at school to find a gathering of his fellow classmates, all Jewish, outside the door.

"We're not allowed in school anymore," one of them informed him. "No Jews. They said go home."

"Then what are you waiting for?" Thomas had said. The others had lingered, as if hoping to find out it was all a mistake. Burying his hurt inside of himself, Thomas had been the first to turn and leave.

It didn't matter that the first-class passengers who were allowed on the upper deck were also Jewish—it nevertheless made him flush with anger. He still hated any rules that separated people into categories.

"Kurt, he can come in."

The man who had spoken was the same young steward who had shown Thomas and Herr Kleist to the cabin.

"But, Manfred, he's tourist-class," Kurt said.

"Captain's orders. Living quarters and dining rooms are to stay separate, but otherwise everyone is free to come and go as they like."

Kurt's lips curled. "I guess they *are* all Jews."

Thomas took a step forward. "So I can go?"

"Of course," Manfred said, showing the way with an outstretched hand.

Thomas did a lap of the deck. He had imagined it would be mostly open space, but it was surprisingly cluttered with deck chairs, lifeboats, ventilation shafts, pipes, and crates of equipment. Thomas heard music coming from the other side of the ship. He turned a corner to see a full band playing. He shook his head—the band made it seem like a joyous departure when in truth they were all escaping by the skin of their teeth. Thomas went to the railing, which was chest-high. He looked down at crew members on the quayside taking care of last-minute details of baggage and supplies. There seemed to be quite a lot being loaded aboard, but Thomas couldn't understand why. Jews were allowed to take very few possessions out of the country. When his neighbors had left a year earlier, the German travel agency had helped them put their furniture and china into storage with the assurance it would all be sent along later. The neighbors had since written to Thomas's mother to say none of it had ever arrived.

Passengers trickled onto the deck until no room was left along the railing. The crew below uncoiled the hawsers, thick as Thomas's waist, from the bollards. The ship began to move as tugboats pulled it into the harbor. The band stopped and everyone waited in expectant silence. The ship's engine coughed up diesel fumes, and Thomas breathed through his mouth to avoid the smell.

Next to Thomas a woman turned her face into her husband's chest and wept. "It's not home anymore," her husband tried to reassure her. "There's nothing to miss."

Other people clapped and cheered. One couple danced. Thomas felt the urge to yell out to his mother, even though she was likely long gone. In his mind he saw the apartment: the leather furniture, the spot by the window where the sun streamed through in the afternoon and where he liked to sit and read. He closed his eyes and felt the ship moving. He wanted to go back—he wanted to jump overboard and swim ashore. He put his hand in his pocket to find the pawn. Feeling its edges calmed him.

Around him people made comments in voices loud enough to be heard by many:

"We're safe."

"They're rid of us."

"Not *all* of us."

A man with a woolen scarf wrapped dramatically around his neck pronounced, *"Let us plunge ourselves into the roar of time, the whirl of accident: may pain and pleasure, success and failure, shift as they will—it's only action that can make a man."*

Thomas recognized the quotation from *Faust*. His parents had an extensive collection of Goethe's works, and Thomas had read the books even when he didn't have to for school. He especially liked Goethe's dramas, because each time he read a play he understood it in a different way. There were so many layers to the language, plot, and characters. Just as with chess, there was always something new to discover that hadn't been there the time before.

The ship lurched out of the harbor, picking up speed. The diesel smell faded, but the vibration of the engine grew so that Thomas could feel it under his feet through the wooden deck. The wind picked up, blowing women's skirts and men's hats. Thomas stared at the water below him and the land, which still seemed very close.

Then, in what seemed like only an instant, the shoreline was gone and black water surrounded them. Thomas felt a wave of claustrophobia and steadied himself on the railing. Once it passed, he turned from the railing and noticed two girls in frilly white dresses. Their parents stood nearby; the father was the man in the scarf who had quoted from *Faust*. The mother wore a showy party dress unlike any

Thomas had ever seen his own mother wear. It made Thomas sad to see the parents standing close together, the girls giggling. They were all together. They were happy. Thomas looked back to sea. It had only been a matter of minutes and yet now Germany was gone. The apartment was gone. His mother was gone. How had they gotten so far away so fast?

The steward Thomas now knew as Manfred walked by, and the elder of the girls stopped him. "Excuse me, could you tell us where the pool is?"

Thomas studied Manfred more closely. He could only be a few years older than Thomas himself: eighteen, nineteen at most. The one fault Thomas could find in his looks was a protruding Adam's apple. He also noticed that his hands seemed to tremble ever so slightly.

"Looking for an evening swim, are you?" Manfred said.

The girls giggled again. "No, but maybe tomorrow."

"The pool isn't up yet. It'll be on A Deck, filled once we get to the Gulf Stream. You wouldn't want to swim in this freezing water."

"Thank you," the older girl said. She grabbed her sister's hand. "This is going to be such fun!"

Thomas shook his head as the girls beamed at each other. "You make it sound like we're on holiday." He hadn't meant to say those words aloud, and now the older girl had turned and was staring at him.

"Well, it's almost like a holiday. We're celebrating."

"Celebrating what?"

"Getting out, of course."

Thomas huffed. "You actually think this"—he glanced up at the swastika flag flapping in the wind—"is getting out?"

"Two weeks' time and we'll be in Cuba. Then we're headed to America. We've already applied for visas. We have an uncle there."

"That's nice for you," Thomas said.

"Where are you and your family eventually going?"

"It's just me."

The girl touched her curly hair. "You're traveling alone?"

"Yes." Thomas thought he might have to suffer through her pitying looks, but instead came an invitation: "You should have dinner with us, then."

Before he could say no, she pulled her father's hand. "Vati, this young man is traveling alone. Can we invite him to dine with us?"

The man with the scarf turned. Streaks of gray in his dark hair gave him a striking appearance.

Thomas might have been too outspoken at times but he wasn't raised without manners. He extended his hand to the man. "Thomas Werkmann."

"Nice to meet you. I'm Professor Affeldt." He motioned to his wife, who was still looking out over the railing. "That is my wife and these are my daughters, Priska and Marianne."

The girls had the same round faces and corkscrew curls, although Priska, the older one, had shorter hair.

"Of course you'll eat with us," Professor Affeldt added.

"That isn't necessary," Thomas replied.

"Are you first-class?"

Thomas shook his head and tried to look appropriately disappointed, since he already knew tourist-class wasn't allowed in the first-class dining room.

"Do you have a dinner jacket?"

"Yes, but—"

"Good. It shouldn't be a problem. We'll say you're a cousin. There are so many families here . . . in fact, aren't we all family now, in a way?"

The girls nodded. Priska smiled and elbowed her sister. "See, I told you we'd make lots of new friends, Marianne."

Thomas opened his mouth, but he couldn't think of any excuse to get himself out of dining with them. For the night anyway, he was stuck.

Chapter Three

✦

How Thomas wished his mother were there to fuss over his clothes now! Was his tie straight? Did his jacket fit? His mother had insisted he pack his father's dinner jacket. She had combed through his father's clothes and picked out several items for Thomas to bring with him. To him it hadn't felt right—it had felt like admitting his father wasn't coming back, something Thomas wasn't ready to do.

"You never know when you might be invited to dine first-class," his mother had said. And she had been right.

Thomas expected the sleeves of the jacket to be too long and the shoulders to be too wide. His father had been of medium build, but nevertheless he had always seemed big to Thomas. Now he realized that they were close to the same size. This knowledge filled him with a pang of regret—he was bound to grow a few more inches, which meant he would soon be taller than his father.

"Where do you think you're going, all dressed up?" Herr Kleist said as he woke from a snooze to find Thomas examining himself in the shaving mirror above the washbasin.

"That's not your concern, remember," Thomas replied. He had made up his mind to have as little to do with Herr Kleist as he could, but he was beginning to think that it would be hard, considering they shared such a small space. He hoped his other two roommates would be at least a bit of a buffer. Before going on deck to look out as the ship departed, he had met them briefly: Oskar and Elias Goldschmid were brothers, university students from Stuttgart.

Herr Kleist grunted and rolled away from Thomas.

Thomas straightened his navy blue tie once more. His face looked too angular in the shaving mirror—all sharp lines and severe points. He smiled at himself to see if it made his face look more pleasant, but then he returned his lips to their usual flat line. Why did he care what he looked like? He didn't want to dine with the Affeldts in the first place. He couldn't bear to look at their happy, smiling faces all night long.

Thomas headed for the door. When he came upstairs to the first-class dining room, he was breathing hard from the flights of stairs and from nerves about the meal ahead. He peered into the half-full dining room, trying to steady his breathing. The tables were set with white linen table-cloths and crystal glasses. Waiters in white coats and black ties scurried from table to table.

"I'm dining with the Affeldt family," he told the hostess once he had summoned the courage to actually enter the room.

"Yes, the cousin," said the woman, who was dressed in a black gown. "Right this way."

Thomas followed her over the gleaming black-and-white checkered floor to the Affeldts' table. Except for the slight vibration underfoot that made the fresh flowers on every table tremble, Thomas would have thought he was at one of the finest restaurants in Berlin.

"Thomas, welcome," Professor Affeldt said, standing to greet him.

Thomas thanked him for the invitation to join them and sat down in the open seat next to Priska. He remembered his posture, straightening in his chair.

"Isn't this grand?" Priska said as she surveyed the room and the well-dressed passengers. She turned to look at her mother. "Mutti, grand, isn't it?"

"Yes, grand," Frau Affeldt said with little emotion. She had curly hair like her daughters but her complexion was pale, almost unhealthy.

The meal began with caviar and toast, crudités and olives.

"I guess they've never had a ship full of Jews before,"

Professor Affeldt said as the caviar was placed in front of him.

"We don't keep kosher," Priska said to Thomas. "Do you?"

"No." He glanced at the nearby tables—some people were eating the caviar, others pushed their plates away. Thomas had seen the kosher shops in Berlin, but he didn't know exactly what people who kept kosher could or couldn't eat. He had never really thought much about it, but now he was curious. Still, he didn't want to ask and risk seeming dim.

Priska passed her olives to her sister. "Marianne loves olives. Isn't that odd?"

"Vati says I have incredibly cultured taste for a ten-year-old," Marianne said.

Priska rolled her eyes. "No, you just have a bottomless stomach."

Thomas himself had never had olives or caviar, but his mother had taught him about both. He knew he was to eat the olives with a fork, not with his fingers, and to return the pits discreetly to his small dinner plate with his fork. He knew that even if he found the caviar delicious, he should only take a teaspoon or two at a time—that there was nothing more gauche than gorging yourself. In fact, his mother had taught him how to eat almost any food imaginable: artichokes and oysters, pistachio nuts and lobster. At the time he had thought she was crazy, but she insisted that he be knowledgeable about the finest things in case he was ever put in a situation where ignorance would bring embarrassment. He had the feeling that she herself had grown up privileged, eating all sorts of fancy foods, but she never liked to talk about her life before she had met his father. All he knew was that she had left that life and her family behind and that her parents hadn't approved of her marrying a Jew, especially a Jew who had been married before, even if he was a widower.

Next the waiter brought salads of iceberg lettuce and cucumbers. Thomas chewed slowly and sipped his water in between bites. He noticed that Frau Affeldt had not touched any of her food.

"So tell us your story," Professor Affeldt said.

Thomas swallowed carefully. "What story is that?"

"Where you're from. How you came to be traveling alone."

Priska explained, "My father's a professor of German literature. Everything's a story to him."

"*Was* a professor of German literature," Professor Affeldt corrected. "Before I was removed from my post."

Thomas hurried through the pertinent details: "I'm from Berlin. After *Reichskristallnacht* my father was declared an enemy of the state, and he went into hiding. Later he was discovered and sent to a *Konzentrationslager*. As for my mother, we only had enough money for one fare." Thomas wasn't good at stories, nor did he want to share what had happened. It seemed to him that there were two kinds of people—the kind who relived every moment of the past in painful detail, and the kind who moved on and never looked back. He wanted to be the kind who moved on. It was one of the first lessons his father had taught him about chess: If you make a poor move, don't dwell on it and let it ruin the rest of your game.

A waiter came over and removed the empty plates. *"Hat es nicht geschmeckt?"* he asked Frau Affeldt.

"I'm not very hungry," she replied.

The waiter frowned and retreated, but he mumbled loud enough to be heard, "No taste, these Jews. Some of them won't even eat *caviar.*"

The Affeldts and Thomas sat in silence. Under his fancy jacket, Thomas felt hot. Professor Affeldt sighed and raised his eyebrows as if to say there was nothing they could do but pretend they hadn't heard the man.

"Your mother had no choice but to send you alone," he said, taking his wife's hand. Thomas could see him appreciating his own family's lot in life—how it could have been even worse. Like Thomas's family, they might have had to split up to escape.

"You must miss your parents terribly," Frau Affeldt offered. "I'm so sorry, Thomas."

It was the first time she had spoken more than just a few words and the first time she had really acknowledged him. He was surprised to find her voice clear and confident.

"Yes, I do." At his words, Thomas felt a stab inside him again. He wondered when, or if, that would go away. "A professor of German literature," Thomas said. "That explains the Goethe you quoted as we left shore."

Professor Affeldt cocked his head at Thomas.

"*It's only action that can make a man . . .* from *Faust*," said Thomas.

"Well done," Professor Affeldt said.

Thomas explained, "My parents have a large collection of Goethe."

"Vati's always quoting Goethe or Schiller or Grillparzer," Priska said. "And he makes us memorize it too." She looked up at the ceiling and quoted: "*As soon as you trust yourself, you will know how to live.* That's from *Faust* too."

Professor Affeldt gave Priska a sidelong glance of approval and then asked Thomas, "Have you had any news of your father?"

"Last we heard he was in Dachau, but that was many months ago now." Thomas shifted in his seat, making sure he felt his father's pawn in his pocket.

The same waiter returned and delivered the next course: chicken bouillon and egg drop soup with vegetables. He placed the delicate china bowls in front of them with quick movements, as if he didn't want to be near them at all. The only time he paused was when he served Priska. He stared at her a moment too long, looking from her face to her chest, and then back up to her face again. She dipped her chin and averted her eyes. The waiter cleared his throat and retreated.

Thomas witnessed this brief moment and saw Priska as the waiter had seen her. It dawned on him that the waiter had stared at her because she was beautiful. Thomas had been too distracted by the ship and leaving home before, but now he saw her clearly: the smoothness of her skin, her bright eyes, the swell of her breasts under the frilly white dress.

She looked up at Thomas and their eyes met. She smiled and returned to eating her soup.

Priska ate in a polite and reserved manner, while Marianne hurried spoonfuls to her mouth. Frau Affeldt didn't lift her spoon.

Professor Affeldt wiped his mouth with the linen napkin. "What was your father's profession?"

"Our family owned a printing press."

"Was it shut down after the boycott?"

"No, my mother isn't Jewish, so she became the face of the shop, while my father and I stayed in the back room."

"And in Cuba?" Professor Affeldt asked.

"My brother's there. He's ten years older than I am. Half brother, actually."

Thomas wished he hadn't mentioned that Walter was not his full brother. How could there be such a thing as half of a person? People shouldn't ever be divided up in such a way.

"We're from Dresden," Priska said. "We had a wonderful life before Herr Hitler. Our nice house, our cat, school, friends. I know there's no such thing as perfect but it was pretty close, wasn't it, Marianne?"

Marianne wiped a dribble of soup from her chin. Her bowl was empty. "I miss Alfie."

"That's our cat," Priska informed Thomas. "We had to leave him with a neighbor. We'll get a new cat in America. And a new house, and we'll go to school again. And we've already made new friends aboard the ship." Priska smiled at Thomas. It made him uncomfortable and he looked away. Who was this girl to be so happy?

The waiter descended again, filling wineglasses and delivering what by Thomas's count was the fourth course. "Rack of veal with potato croquettes and asparagus in a reduction sauce," the waiter announced through tight lips, with another hungry glance at Priska's chest.

"I don't want a new cat. I want Alfie," Marianne said.

"Alfie loved Marianne best. He slept in her bed at night," Priska explained. "Did you have lots of friends in Berlin, Thomas?"

"Some," he said, though for the most part it had always been the three of them—his mother, his father, and Thomas—a tight little cocoon, even before Hitler.

"This veal is delightful. Very tender," Professor Affeldt said, looking at his wife. "You should try it, *mein Schatz.*"

To Thomas he explained that Frau Affeldt's stomach had been unsettled ever since they had left shore.

"That's been the hardest part for me . . . leaving my friends," Priska said.

Thomas closed his eyes for a moment. If leaving her friends behind was the worst Priska had been through, then she didn't know real pain. Thomas opened his eyes and glanced at the people around them, commenting on the delicious food, raising a glass in a toast. He wanted to stand up and shout for it all to stop, this pretending everything was magically better, that they were safe. There was no such thing as safe.

The rack of veal was followed by baked young duck. Dessert was three courses in itself: apricot compote, maraschino ice cream with vanilla cookies, and finally a plate of Swiss and herbed cheeses. Marianne ate almost every bite of all the courses. When Thomas commented on her healthy appetite, Professor Affeldt and Priska shared a look and then laughed.

"That's our little girl," Professor Affeldt said.

It was the best food Thomas had eaten in his whole life. As he went back to his cabin, his stomach gluttonously full, he thought of the sparse meal his mother had likely eaten for dinner that night.

Each level of the ship he descended, the engine's vibration increased. He used the W.C. down the hall and then returned to the cabin. Oskar's and Elias's beds were empty. Herr Kleist was asleep, and he hadn't even bothered to draw the privacy curtain. Thomas climbed into his bunk and pulled the curtain around him. But privacy was not to be had. Below him Herr Kleist added to the vibrations with his snoring. At home Thomas had slept on a daybed in the sitting room of the small apartment. Often he would have to go to sleep in his parents' bed because they would be up late in the sitting room with friends, planning how to get the information they collected to other countries. His parents had been part of a resistance group for almost as long as Thomas could remember. But instead of distributing anti-Hitler leaflets or participating in acts of sabotage, they worked to convince other countries that not everyone in Germany believed in the Nazis and that many would welcome a revolution. Sometimes his parents would catch a few hours of sleep on the daybed; sometimes they didn't sleep at all. He missed his parents and the apartment where he'd lived his whole life terribly.

Thomas turned to face the wall and put the pillow over his head, but he could still hear Herr Kleist droning. After a few more moments, he decided that instead of trying to force sleep, he would venture back up to the top deck. Once outside, he stood by the railing, watching the black water rustle and churn below.

"Thomas?"

He startled, forgetting that anyone on board even knew his name, and turned to find Priska.

"What are you doing up here?" he asked. He had imagined her tucked happily into bed, her mother and father having kissed her good night.

"I came to see the moon," she said.

Thomas looked up. It was a sharp sliver tonight, bright and gleaming. The stars were overwhelming themselves, so many of them, like minnows of the sky. Thomas had once been the very type of person who noticed the moon and stars and sunlight and flowers. But over the past year he'd stopped caring so much about the world. In fact, it felt wrong that flowers budded and the moon cycled when everything else had turned crazy around him.

Priska looked at the sky. "*Night is the other half of life, and the better half.* That's from Goethe too—*Wilhelm Meister's Apprenticeship.*"

Thomas rolled his eyes. "Have you read Goethe, or do you just memorize certain parts for your father?"

"I've read plenty but I don't love it like my father does. He was writing a study on Goethe before the *Reichskulturkammer* put an end to any Jew publishing a book. Marianne is named after the actress Wilhelm Meister falls in love with. My father wanted to name me Gretchen—"

"From *Faust,*" Thomas said. He had to acknowledge

that the name might suit her. Gretchen was the one woman whose beauty Faust would sell his soul to the devil for.

Priska nodded. "Thankfully, Mutti insisted I be named after her favorite aunt and not a woman who kills her illegitimate child, goes insane, and is condemned to death! My favorite books are *Gone with the Wind* and *The Good Earth*. Here my father is a professor of German literature and I love American books!" Priska looked up at the moon again. "By the way, what are *you* doing on deck so late at night?"

Thomas shrugged. "Couldn't sleep."

"And you don't have anyone to worry if you're not in bed."

Thomas looked away. He was well aware he didn't have anyone to care for him, but hearing it so plainly stung nonetheless.

"I just mean it was easy for you," she said quickly. "I had to wait until Marianne was asleep and then tiptoe out. Luckily she sleeps like she eats, like an elephant." When Thomas didn't reply, she asked, "Did you like having dinner with us?"

"It was very nice of you to invite me," he answered. He didn't think he could tell her that being with her family made him miss his own even more.

Priska blinked but she continued to hold his gaze. The wind blew her hair around her face. "I can't wait till the pool is up, can you?"

He paused before asking, "How do you do it?"

"Do what?"

"Be so happy all the time."

Priska glanced at the sky. The moon had slipped behind a cloud. "I guess . . . ," she began, but Thomas heard voices and he stopped listening to her. He turned his head toward the voices so she would understand that he was trying to listen in.

A man asked, "How many ships?"

"What is it?" Priska whispered to Thomas.

"Shh," he told her.

Another man answered the first. "Two. They both left at about the same time we did, but they're smaller and faster. If they get there first, the quotas for Cuba might be full and then who knows what will happen. We'll likely be stuck dragging these Jews back to Germany."

Thomas heard footsteps coming toward them. He took Priska's hand and pulled her behind a ventilation shaft. The men walked by. He recognized one of them as Kurt, the officer who had tried to keep him off the first-class deck.

"This is no ordinary tourist cruise, that's for sure," the other officer said to Kurt. He was dressed in the same Nazi Party uniform as Kurt.

"Not when we're asked to treat swine like royalty," Kurt answered. "I don't care what the captain says, it'll be quite a feat if I can keep looking at them without spitting."

Thomas glanced at Priska; her face looked pinched,

as if she were wincing. He was almost glad to overhear their talk. It confirmed what he had known from the start—that they were on a ship with a crew composed of their greatest enemies and that arriving safely in Cuba was not a guarantee.

The men continued across the deck, their voices fading. Thomas realized he hadn't let go of Priska's hand. He quickly released it.

"See," he whispered. "Everyone acts like we're in the clear. But you heard them, you heard what they said."

"So they don't like us," she replied. "After we dock in Cuba, we won't ever have to see them or another Nazi again."

Certain that the men were gone, Thomas came out from behind the ventilation shaft, and Priska followed him. "What I don't understand is why the charade? Why not just treat us like they did back home?"

Priska pushed her hair back from her face. "Vati says it's the captain's orders. He heard that the captain doesn't believe in any of the laws and as long as it's his ship, he won't have us treated differently than any other passenger. Vati says he isn't even a Party member."

Thomas clucked, still unconvinced. "I think I'd rather be treated poorly—then I'd know where I stand. And now there are two other ships. Like those men said, what if we get to Cuba and they're over the quota numbers?"

The moon had peeked back out, and it shed enough

light for Thomas to see Priska's hair bounce as the wind blew it against her shoulders. Even her curly hair seemed carefree, not like his mother's heavy, straight hair.

"Other ships are going the same way. I don't see why that's a problem," she said. "We have landing permits. That means we are *permitted* to land. We don't need to be worried about quotas anymore."

Thomas remembered how his mother and father had worried constantly about quota numbers. They spent hours discussing how many Jews every conceivable country, from Switzerland to Spain to South Africa, would possibly take.

Thomas sighed. "If it's not a problem, then why were they talking about it?"

"I don't know."

"Right," Thomas said, "you *don't* know."

Chapter Four

Thomas was determined to learn his way around the ship, to etch a permanent map of it in his mind. He imagined someday drawing it out for his mother or father to see. He knew this was just a fantasy, that it would likely never happen, but he let himself imagine it anyway. He walked from bow to stern, from starboard to port, from lower deck to upper. He found out that the first-class cabins were closest to sea level—and also farthest, he noted, from the droning of the engine. The best rooms opened straight onto the deck. Thomas passed men and women taking their daily constitutional or relaxing in lounge chairs. A man whizzed by on roller skates, nearly knocking Thomas over. At the stern was the smoking room, where mostly men chatted over coffee and played cards. Everyone on the ship seemed busy doing something normal—no one seemed concerned with whether they would make it to Cuba.

On the sports deck, Thomas saw a group playing shuffleboard.

"Thomas!"

He heard his name and lifted his head, coming out of his own thoughts. It was Priska, shuffleboard cue in one hand, waving to him.

He had just assumed that after he had been short with her the night before, she would have decided that he wouldn't be a good friend. But there she was, waving like he had never snapped at her in the first place.

He walked over and stood with a few of the other players. "Your turn," said the girl Priska was playing with. She had brown hair and her face was covered in freckles. Before Priska took her shot, the girl whispered something in her ear that made Priska laugh and shout, "Oh, Ingrid!"

Thomas was content to watch, but a boy who looked about his own age said, "We're playing teams next. You can be on my team if you want."

"I don't play," Thomas said. He wondered how they could have formed what seemed like a tight-knit group in just over a day.

"You mean you don't know how?" the boy asked. "It's not hard."

Priska pushed the disk with the cue. The disk landed in

one of the marked boxes and the boy called out, "That's ten points off!" He turned back to Thomas and explained, "That's the only one you don't want to get it in." He wiped his hand on his pants and then offered it to Thomas. "My name's Günther."

"Thomas."

"Nice to meet you." He smiled, revealing small, straight teeth. His hair was thick, which made his skullcap sit funny on top of his head.

In the next round of the game, Priska landed in a high-point triangle. Marianne clapped. She stood on the side with another young girl Thomas soon learned was Hannelore. Both girls wore short pants with socks pulled up to their knees. Ingrid knocked Priska's disk out of the triangle with her turn. "Sorry," Ingrid said, grinning.

Priska tossed her head and stuck out her tongue at Ingrid. The match continued. By the end, Priska had won.

"Now it's boys against girls," Priska announced, looking at Thomas.

"You sure you won't play?" Günther asked Thomas. "It's easy to catch on."

"No thank you," Thomas replied.

"Come on," Priska cajoled.

Thomas shook his head and Priska stuck out her lips in an exaggerated pout. A part of him did want to join in. A part of him wanted to laugh with them, to not care about whether he knew how to play or not. It was as if chess had ruined him for casual games in a way. He took everything too seriously.

"Well, it's me and Jakob, then," Günther said.

Ingrid's younger brother's face lit up and he went to join Günther.

On the first round Günther landed in a high-point triangle, and then Priska sent the disk flying past in the hope of knocking him out of the way.

"She was out to get you, Günther," Ingrid said.

Manfred came by and must have witnessed the shot, because he called to Priska, "You need a lesson!"

Everyone stopped what they were doing and turned to look at him.

Priska shrugged. "It's fun like this."

"But it'll be more fun if you knock all the boys out of the way." He moved onto the court. "You need to push more from your body, not just use your arm." He stepped toward her. "May I?"

Without waiting for an answer, he took the cue.

Günther eased off to the side. Ingrid followed. Moments before, Ingrid had been giggling, but now her face was serious. Marianne and Hannelore stood quietly on the side too.

Manfred demonstrated how to use more body than arm strength, knocking Günther's disk on the first try. Thomas wanted to tell Manfred he was doing nothing but ruining what had been a fun game. Manfred placed the cue back in

Priska's hands. Then he put his hands on her waist. Heat rose up Thomas's neck. He thought of the way the waiter's eyes had traveled to Priska's chest and lingered there. He too would surely have loved any excuse to touch her. Thomas hated how the Nazis could touch and take whatever they wanted.

"Like this," Manfred said. "Turn your shoulders to face where you want to send the disk. Yes, good. Now pick up your eyes from the disk and use your body to push. . . ."

"Oh, I see," Priska replied, offering what Thomas hoped was a fake smile. She stood upright and stiff. "Thank you."

"You'll be winning in no time, showing all these boys who's in charge!"

He stepped back and the playing tentatively resumed. But still no one smiled or joked.

Thomas expected Manfred to leave but instead he came over and stood next to him. There was that heat again— Thomas wondered if his face was as red as it felt. The foot of space between them seemed much too little, but before Thomas could move away, Manfred came even closer. He elbowed Thomas gently. It would have been a harmless, chummy gesture among friends. But to Thomas it felt like a subtle statement of power—only Manfred could elbow Thomas. Thomas could never have elbowed Manfred.

Manfred said in a quiet voice, "She's very beautiful, isn't she?"

Thomas followed Manfred's gaze to Priska. He swallowed, trying to tame his anger. He remembered a knock at the door of the print shop, a Nazi officer questioning his mother, looking her up and down. Thomas had watched, knowing his father, who was hiding in the back room, would risk his life if he came out. Thomas often wondered what would have happened if the officer had tried to do anything to his mother. Would Thomas have moved to stop him? Would his father have come out, no matter what the consequences?

Thomas looked up to see a man wearing a Nazi uniform coming toward them. He was tall and heavy-set, with a stubby nose and dark rings under his eyes. He limped ever so slightly and walked with a cane. Thomas thought it strange that a Party officer who used a cane would be on board a ship. Didn't you need legs of steel?

The man stopped and saluted Manfred. "*Heil Hitler*. Is everything all right here?"

Manfred straightened. "Yes, sir."

The man hesitated a few moments before leaving. Soon after, Manfred nodded at Priska and the rest of the group.

"Well, enjoy yourself," he said, and headed off.

Bothered again by the ship's vibration and Herr Kleist's snoring, Thomas went back to the upper deck that night. He was grateful for the fresh air and relative quiet. If the ventilation shafts on the top deck actually fed fresh air to the lower decks, it most certainly didn't reach Thomas's cabin. He breathed deeply, clearing his head.

People came and went: a couple holding hands, a group of young men, including Thomas's bunkmates Oskar and Elias. The night before they had come to bed long after the deck lights were extinguished, smelling of cigarettes and alcohol. Even once they were in their bunks, they talked in passionate yet hushed voices about Rosa Luxemburg and Karl Liebknecht. They spoke of Luxemburg's last words before she was executed for being a founding member of the Communist Party, how she had predicted that the masses would indeed bring a revolution to Germany. Thomas had lain awake listening, reminded of the many nights he'd listened to his parents and their friends in heated discussion. Sometimes they had argued about how best to fight Hitler's regime. Someone would speak up in favor of a plan for sabotage or inform them of rumors of a *putsch* against Hitler, but Thomas's father always said they could never overthrow the Nazi Party without help from outside forces.

At every noise Thomas hoped he'd look up to find Priska. But why should she come up to the top deck again? They had made no promises to meet. He hadn't even been particularly nice to her. Thomas scratched at the top wooden rail. The wood was almost spongy. From the outside the ship had looked flawless, but up close he saw that the salty air took its toll. He had just about given up on Priska and was considering going back to his cabin when he saw her walking toward him.

"I was wondering if I'd find you up here again tonight," she said.

She joined him by the railing and looked down at the sea. "I asked my father about the other ships. He said it shouldn't be a problem, but I could tell it made him nervous. When he's nervous, he never looks me in the eye. He just doesn't want me to worry. Have you heard anything else?"

"No, it's been quiet up here. If we really want to find out anything, we have to go looking."

Priska drew back from the railing. "All right. Where do we look?"

He hadn't really meant for her to join him, and he hadn't even been serious about investigating at all, but now he felt compelled. And at her words a shot of adrenaline rushed through him, like when his mother and father would talk of an operation. After his parents gathered information, they figured out ways to get it to government officials in other countries whom they had managed to contact. They usually asked someone who was new to the group to carry the information. That way, if the person was caught and tortured, he or she would have only so much knowledge to reveal. Thomas had always wished he could take part. He imagined elaborate scenarios where they would need a kid to go where adults couldn't.

Thomas said to Priska, "We would need to go where the crew are. They're the ones who will know about the other ships."

"Maybe the dining room," Priska suggested. "They'll be cleaning up."

"We can try it for a start."

The last guests were trailing out of the dining room, commenting on the savory dessert of California peaches and raspberry ice cream.

A young couple passed by them. "They're newlyweds, Paul and Claudia," Priska told Thomas. Paul had his arm around Claudia. Claudia leaned against him as they walked. "They're always holding hands or kissing," Priska continued. "Don't they make a handsome couple?"

Thomas shrugged. "I guess."

Priska stared at them as they walked away. She laid her hand across her heart and sighed. "Look how in love they are."

The tables inside the dining room had all been cleared and looked strangely bare. The only noise came from the staff chattering and dishes clanging. Thomas and Priska slipped inside and stood near the door to the kitchen. Thomas leaned forward and peeked through the round window in the door. He could see the cups and bowls hanging in a line from hooks on the ceiling.

"Some of these Jews didn't touch their food," a man

said. "I thought they were supposed to be greedy, the type to lick a plate clean."

"That's only when it comes to money," another replied, and they both laughed.

Thomas glanced at Priska, who shook her head. The talk continued but it was mostly about everyday things: family, girlfriends, the weather.

After a few minutes Thomas and Priska exchanged another look, and then Priska leaned close and whispered, "What's next?"

Thomas motioned for Priska to follow him. Back out by the stairwell, he stopped. "We need to go where the real crew is. The ones who sail the ship, not the ones who scrub the dishes."

"Like to their sleeping quarters?"

"Exactly," Thomas said. He had explored what he could of the ship, but the crew's quarters and engine room were off-limits to passengers, and he had no idea where they slept. He felt sure that their nighttime expedition had come to a close and was surprised by Priska's response.

"I know where they sleep. My mother and I were looking for the beauty salon and we got terribly lost." She looked at him, waiting for his answer.

"Let's go," he said, feeling as if he had to live up to her expectations.

As they headed down the stairwell, Thomas wondered

if Priska was as short of breath as he was. For a moment he thought of his parents again, and he imagined them coming to him late at night, telling him they needed him for a very important, dangerous mission. He would need to go to England and deliver information to Neville Chamberlain himself. Would he have been too scared to do it? How could he have when his chest felt tight even now?

Priska led and Thomas followed. He watched her back, waiting for her to suddenly stop and tell him she'd changed her mind. She could say she was worried her parents might come to check on her and notice she was gone, or that Marianne might wake up and find her missing.

But soon they were down in the bowels of the ship, standing in the dimly lit passage outside the crew's quarters. The air smelled of sweat, mildew, and machine oil. They heard laughter and then what sounded like men playing cards. It was hard to make out their words from the far side of the passage.

"We should go closer," Thomas whispered.

Priska nodded. If she was even the slightest bit scared, Thomas couldn't tell. If caught, they would claim to be lost, but would it be a good-enough excuse? And for Priska, being found outside the crew's bunk room at such an unrespectable hour could have scandalous implications.

Thomas moved closer to the door of the bunk room, trying to ignore his heart thundering in his chest. He reminded himself he was supposed to be the fearless one.

Outside the door was a bulletin board, on which news-paper clippings from *Der Stürmer* were posted. "Com-plete lies devised to defame us," his father had said about the Nazi newspaper when Thomas had first seen it in one of the display cases put up by the Reich. It had a cartoon depicting a Jew with a grotesquely exaggerated nose and lips, politely asking someone to make room for him to sit on a park bench. The next frame showed the Jewish man shoving the other man off the bench. The text that went with the cartoon explained that this was how Jews be-haved in all situations, not just when it came to park benches.

The clippings they looked at now were dated only days before the ship had sailed. Dark, grainy photos showed grim-looking men, heads shaven and scowling.

Priska pointed to one of the men. "Wait, that man—"

"Shh," Thomas told her.

He read the caption underneath to himself: *Germany rids itself of scourge of the earth. Savage criminals leave on ship headed to Cuba.* Thomas shuddered. He knew what the Nazis thought of them, so why did it always feel like a kick in the gut? Why did it always hurt all over again? Once again he found himself asking why the Nazis put them on this ship to begin with. If they believed Jews were the "scourge of the earth," why were they serving them caviar and veal? Could it really be on the captain's or-ders alone?

Thomas had started to read the accompanying article when he heard footsteps.

"Go," Thomas whispered, and they ran down the passage and back up the stairwell to the top deck. He listened to hear if anyone was following them, but it was quiet. Outside they stood still, catching their breath. Finally Priska said, "That man in the photo . . . the one with the shaved head? That was Günther's father. I'm sure of it. Günther's mother managed to get him released from Sachsenhausen on the promise that he'd leave Germany within three months. Many on this ship promised the same thing."

Her words hit Thomas low in the stomach. Why hadn't his mother been able to get his father out of Dachau?

"It said he was a criminal but his only crime was trying to help people. He's a doctor, and when the Nazis said Jews couldn't practice medicine anymore, he kept seeing patients. What was he to do, turn away people who needed treatment?"

"Those papers are full of lies," Thomas said. "They make us out to be criminals so everyone in Germany will be glad to get rid of us. And people believe it too. They want us gone."

"Not everyone feels that way," Priska said.

"*Everyone,*" Thomas said.

"Surely there are still some decent people in the world, and if they—"

"No," Thomas cut her off. "You can't think like that.

You can't trust anyone. We had close family friends, the Levins. The Levins had neighbors, a nice old couple. When the laws were issued saying that Jews were no longer German citizens, the neighbors came to the Levins and said they didn't care about the laws, that the Levins would always be Germans to them and were always welcome at their home. Frau Levin went over for tea with the old lady almost daily. They were close friends. Then one day the Nazis came and ransacked the Levins' house. The Nazis said there were reports that they'd been out after curfew and that they were Communists. They destroyed their furniture and confiscated their china and their jewelry. Then they took Herr Levin away."

Priska looked at the deck. Thomas remembered how she had said her father wouldn't make eye contact when he was nervous about something.

"It was that nice old couple that turned them in . . . their *friends*." Thomas paused and then said, his voice fierce, "There is no one you can trust."

Chapter Five

Thomas stood among the many other passengers at the railing watching the activity below. They had arrived in the Cherbourg harbor to load supplies. Burly men hauled crates of fruits and vegetables up the gangway. A crane lifted the heaviest crates in netting straight onto the ship.

"The cowardly French," Frau Rosen said. She stood a few feet down the railing from Thomas, taking a cigarette from its box.

"You can't blame them alone," Oskar said. He produced a match and lit her cigarette. "Chamberlain signed the papers too."

Frau Rosen exhaled a gust of smoke and said with a roll of her eyes, "Peace for our time. Hardly."

Thomas knew they were talking about the Munich Agreement. Hitler had wanted to take the Sudentenland from Czechoslovakia, and he had been ready to take it by force. The French had an alliance with Czechoslovakia, and Czechoslovakia had counted on France's coming to its defense if Hitler attacked. But instead France and Britain went behind Czechoslovakia's back and brokered an agreement with Hitler. He'd get the Sudentenland and there would be no war—at least for the moment.

Thomas turned to look the other way, down the ship toward the giant funnels. He recognized the ship's captain, who had come to oversee the transfer, by his meticulous uniform. It had eight gold buttons down the front and gold stripes on the sleeves. His pristine white hat had a black brim. Thomas wondered how he kept it so clean, and if he perhaps had several of them. The uniform was missing one very important thing, however: a Party badge on the arm. Priska had been right—he was not a Party member. Thomas didn't quite know how this was possible. Everyone was a member now. Whether they agreed with Nazi ideals or not, it was near suicide not to join. The captain had a thin mustache and a pointy chin. He looked almost severe when, in fact, he was very nice. He said *"Guten Tag"* to every person he passed and even stopped to talk to a few, inquiring how they were finding the voyage so far. As he continued to the gangway, he kept checking his pocket watch.

"How many more crates to be loaded?" he asked one of the crew.

"Not too many. Twenty or so."

He took out his pocket watch again and tapped it lightly with his finger. "Good. We need to get back on the open sea."

Manfred strode up the gangway carrying a big bag. "Good day, Captain," he said. "I've got the mail."

An announcement was broadcast over the ship's loudspeaker that mail could be picked up outside the social hall on the promenade deck. In minutes, passengers surrounded Manfred. Soon all Thomas could see of him was an occasional glimpse of his hand as he held out a letter. Thomas listened to the voices:

"Is there a letter for me? Bermann?"

"My brother-in-law must have written."

Manfred read the names out loud and people hurried away, clutching letters to their chests. Some ripped the letters open on the spot and others retreated to their cabins to pore over their relatives' words in private.

"Werkmann?"

Thomas's body jolted at the sound of his name. Then he remembered there was likely to be more than one Werkmann on a ship of nine hundred. Also, he couldn't imagine who would have written to him. He didn't think his mother would have, and he wasn't expecting to hear from his brother. Manfred searched the faces of the few people left.

"Werkmann, Thomas?"

No one stepped forward and Thomas realized it was for him. For a moment he thought the letter might be from his mother after all, perhaps with news of his father. He held out his trembling hand to Manfred. Manfred didn't release the letter and they stood there, each holding an end.

Manfred said, "Thomas Werkmann." It seemed to Thomas that he was putting a name with Thomas's face.

Thomas hesitated, unsure why Manfred hadn't let go of the letter.

Manfred finally let go as Herr Kleist descended on him. He was breathing heavily, as if he had run from the other side of the ship. "I heard there was mail. There has to be a letter from my son." Herr Kleist gave his name and scowled sideways at Thomas as Manfred checked his empty bag.

"Nothing, sir, I'm sorry."

Herr Kleist straightened his cap. *"Nochmal, bitte schön."*

Manfred offered an apologetic smile but he didn't look in the bag again.

Herr Kleist wiped at his watering eye. "Will we be receiving more mail?"

"This is it until Havana."

Herr Kleist's shoulders sunk. For a moment, in spite of how Herr Kleist had treated him, Thomas felt sorry for him.

"Only twelve more days and we'll be there," Manfred said.

As Herr Kleist pleaded with Manfred to check once more, Thomas drifted off to open his letter. He couldn't bear Herr Kleist's lack of dignity any longer. The envelope felt as thin as the onion skins his mother left on the chopping board. The upright lettering on the envelope seemed strangely familiar to him, although he knew it was not his mother's. She had a more looping script. He felt both relieved and disappointed that it was not news from his mother about his father. It meant there was hope, but it also meant that they still knew nothing. He pulled out a single page. There were only a few lines of text, in the same proper lettering as on the envelope.

Dear Thomas,

I eagerly await your arrival in Havana. I hope the trip is going smoothly. When you get here, we can immediately begin trying to find a way to send for your mother. I don't know what to do about our father. I worry we will never see him again.

Godspeed.

Your brother,
Walter

"Who wrote to you?"

Thomas turned to see Priska peeking over his shoulder. She always seemed to find him, always seemed to sneak up on him.

He drew the letter to his chest. "My brother from Havana."

"What did he say that's so private?"

Thomas was near to being annoyed with her. He wanted a few moments to himself to reread the short note and savor the fact that someone was waiting for him, that someone else in the world cared about him. But he saw Priska grinning at him, and he knew she was only teasing. He decided to play along. "He said that he's waiting for me . . . and our quota numbers have come up and we'll be off to America right away. He has jobs lined up there too." Thomas found a smile creeping onto his face. He was never one to joke or dream, and he was finding it surprisingly fun.

"And a house too?" Priska asked.

"A mansion. In New York City. Right next to the Rockefellers."

Priska laughed. He had made her laugh. But as quickly as Thomas's smile had come, it faded as he looked at the harbor. "Why haven't we left yet? The supplies are all loaded."

"What's the hurry?" Priska leaned against the railing, as if trying to get as close as she could to the land. "It's nice to get a glimpse of the real world for a moment. Look, if you squint you can see the cars and the people all going about their day."

Thomas thought of the captain and how he had kept checking his pocket watch. "The hurry is the other ships. If we waste time here, they'll reach Cuba before us."

Thomas couldn't believe he had to remind her about the ships. Had she plain forgotten, or did she really not see them as a threat to their safe arrival? He didn't understand how she could just assume everything would work out.

"What did your brother really write to you?" Priska asked.

"Only that he's waiting for me and he hopes the trip goes smoothly."

A very pregnant woman walked by, leading a toddler by the hand. The toddler was nearly dragging her doll on the floor, and her mother told her to be more careful and pick it up.

"That's Lisbeth and her daughter, Margot," Priska informed Thomas. "She's due to have the baby any day now. Did you know that if you give birth on a ship, it's common practice to name your child after the ship? Francis is a good-enough name, but what if she were aboard the *Imperator*?"

"I didn't know that," Thomas said, shaking his head at her. She was amazing in the way she befriended people so quickly and learned all about them. He wondered if there was a single person on the ship she didn't know yet.

"How much older is your brother than you?"

"Ten years. He's twenty-five."

"Which makes you fifteen. I'm fourteen but my birthday is in August. When's yours?"

"December."

"When did your brother leave Germany?"

Thomas almost couldn't keep up with her. She jumped from one topic to the next. "Nineteen thirty-four."

Her lips moved slightly as she calculated the math in her head. "When you were ten."

Thomas nodded. "He lived near Nürnberg, so I didn't really know him."

"Why in Nürnberg when you lived in Berlin?"

"You don't quit with the questions, do you?"

Priska grinned. "No."

Thomas explained how his father's first wife had died and his father had moved to Berlin for business. "Walter stayed with my father's first wife's parents. Then my father met my mother and remarried, and by that time Walter was no longer a child and it didn't make sense for him to come live with us."

"Your mother isn't Jewish, but your father is. Do you celebrate Shabbos?"

"No," Thomas said. After a moment's hesitation he asked, "What's it like?"

"Shabbos?"

He nodded.

"It's wonderful. I look forward to it more than anything. Sometimes during the week my father misses dinner or my mother has to visit a friend, but on Shabbos they're both home and we're all together as a family. My mother lights the candles and then we bless the wine, and the challah bread is the most delicious of all."

The lunch gong sounded and Priska laughed. "As if on cue! Come on. Have lunch with us. I think Marianne fancies you. Have you noticed how she can't stop smiling whenever you're around?"

Thomas certainly hadn't noticed. He found himself blushing and then felt silly. Marianne was ten years old—still a child, really. But he had never imagined *anyone* fancying him before. "All right," he said.

Thomas took one more look at the letter before folding it and putting it in his pocket. Once it was out of sight, he realized why the handwriting seemed familiar—it was very similar to his own.

—∾—

At lunch the same waiter kept looking at Priska. He refilled her water glass when it barely needed it, and Thomas was sure it was just so he could get another look at her. Halfway through the meal, Manfred stopped by their table. He stood next to Priska but he addressed Professor Affeldt. "Are you finding everything to your liking so far?"

Professor Affeldt dabbed at his mouth with his napkin. "Yes, thank you."

"As the captain's steward, I was asked specifically by the captain to make sure everyone has everything they need."

"Yes, everything has been wonderful."

Manfred took one more look at Priska and then retreated.

When he was gone, Thomas said, "The captain really isn't a Party member? How is that possible?"

Professor Affeldt shrugged. "Even the Nazis let something slip through the cracks every once in a while. They think *Wilhelm Tell* is such a wonderful example of German nationalism that they put it on at every chance they get. So much for the murder of the tyrant in the end—somehow they overlooked that part!"

"Do you really believe the captain is why we're being treated so well?"

"I suppose so."

Priska smiled at Thomas. "Look who's asking all the questions now!"

Thomas continued, "I still can't understand why they would let us on this ship."

Professor Affeldt pointed out, "They did charge us a lot of money."

"But couldn't they have charged us as much to travel in steerage?"

"I guess we shouldn't ask too many questions, Thomas, but should be grateful for our good fortune." Professor Affeldt added with more flare: *"The day of fortune is like a harvest day. We must be busy when the corn is ripe."*

Thomas nodded. *"Torquato Tasso."*

"You *are* well-read," Professor Affeldt said.

Thomas smiled, reveling in the compliment. Then he saw Priska cast him a sidelong look.

"Thomas is always worrying too much," she said, as if she had known him his whole life.

Thomas managed a smile, but he thought, *And you don't worry enough.*

Chapter Six

The next day Thomas decided to see what people were doing in the smoking room. He saw two men sitting across from each other. One man's shoulders were hunched over, and he was staring intently at the table in front of him. The man sitting across from him was also strangely focused on the table, although he sat straighter in his chair.

Goose bumps rose up Thomas's back and arms. He stepped closer. Yes. There was the board, the black and white squares, the handsome pieces. Thomas's hand immediately traveled to his pocket, and he felt the edges of the pawn. His breathing quickened. The room was hazy with pipe and cigarette smoke, but Thomas knew that was not the cause of his shortness of breath. He moved close enough to see the board fully.

It looked like an odd variation of the Guico Piano.

Black considered his next move. Thomas was already analyzing an interesting move in the position. The first three moves were forced but beyond that it was murkier.

White cleared his throat.

"Yes, yes, I know," said Black, and reached for his rook.

Thomas flinched. He traded rooks. It wasn't losing but he'd missed a better move.

"There was something else I should have done there," Black said, shaking his head at himself.

"You should have taken his bishop," Thomas let slip.

Both men looked up, noticing Thomas for the first time.

"The boy knows chess," White said. He nodded at his friend. "But don't give him too much help or I'll end up losing."

"You always win," Black said. "I don't imagine that will change just because we're not on German soil anymore."

The men shared a laugh. They reminded Thomas of the mismatched tea set his mother owned. The man playing black was mostly bald yet had a thick beard. The man playing white was clean-shaven and had a head of thick white hair. Both looked to be well into their sixties.

Thomas looked up from the board while White figured out his next move. The Nazi officer with the cane was going by the window. Thomas still couldn't imagine why a man with a cane would be assigned to a ship. His father used to tell him that the most important part of resistance work, as of chess, was to trust your intuition. Your intuition would tell you when to be careful. One time his father had canceled a mission at the last minute because he felt that the man who would deliver the report was not trustworthy. When his mother had asked his father why he suspected the man, he had only shaken his head and said, "I don't feel right about him."

Now Thomas's intuition told him something wasn't right about this man. Why use a cane if his limp was so minor in the first place? A boy in their building back home had always been feigning one injury or another: holding his arm to his chest and claiming to have broken it, limping and saying he'd turned his ankle. No matter how hard he tried, none of his injuries ever looked real.

The man shuffled out of sight and Thomas turned his attention back to the board.

The man playing white glanced at Thomas. "Jürgen thinks his queen is the only piece worth moving."

Jürgen took his queen and moved it forward. "I don't have the patience for pawns." He smiled at Thomas before cocking his head at the man playing white. "Wilhelm, you really ought to use your queen more. Minor pieces are much too serious for coffeehouse chess. Leave the slow, methodical play for the tournament players and let's have some action."

Wilhelm shook his head at Jürgen and made a knight move. "You've created too many weaknesses. These knight outposts are going to haunt you pretty soon."

Wilhelm winked at Thomas and then extended his hand. "I'm Wilhelm Oppenheimer, and this patzer is Jürgen Hirshberg."

"Thomas Werkmann."

"So you play?" Wilhelm said.

"Yes," Thomas said.

Other people ambled in and out of the smoking room, snacking on the sandwiches laid out on the sideboard. In one corner of the room a man smoked a pipe and perused the shipboard newspaper, which offered only snippets of world news but was better than nothing. Three other men played cards, wagering on the outcome. Above them a sign read: BEWARE OF CARDSHARPS. Thomas chuckled as he read it. Cardsharps might have made plenty of money scheming innocent players on other voyages but not on this one. The only benefit of having no money in the first place was that you had none to lose. Thomas had been allowed to purchase up to 230 reichsmarks in shipboard money, but anything not spent upon arrival in Havana would be forfeited.

At one point Jürgen's wife came in to tell him he'd forgotten to take his medicine. "I knew I'd find you up here," she chided, dropping two pills into his hand.

Immersed in chess, Thomas lost track of time. Following

the complications of the game, he almost forgot he was on board a ship at all.

The men in the smoking room took notice when Manfred entered. Just the sight of him, after seeing the newspaper clippings with Priska a few nights before, made Thomas's stomach turn. Manfred could pretend to be nice, but Thomas knew how he and the other crew members really felt about Jews.

"Having a good game?" Manfred asked, stopping next to Thomas.

"Yes, thank you," Wilhelm replied in a polite, clipped voice.

"Always, sir," added Jürgen, barely meeting Manfred's glance.

Thomas checked the table nearby where the three men were playing cards. One man folded, then the next. The third swept the coins from the table, but no one shuffled or dealt for the next game. Thomas waited for Manfred to either do something or leave, but he did neither. "This is one of my favorite games," Manfred said to Thomas. "Much better than shuffleboard."

Surely he considered himself an expert at chess too, Thomas thought. Thomas felt a twinge of satisfaction in knowing that in all likelihood he was a much better player than Manfred.

Wilhelm and Jürgen continued their game, but Thomas could tell they were distracted by Manfred. Twice Jürgen made a poor move, cursing himself under his breath. And Wilhelm didn't comment on Jürgen's mistakes. The pace of the game quickened, each player making rapid moves, as if they didn't want to be seen thinking. Jürgen kept glancing up at Manfred and then turning his eyes quickly back to the board. Jürgen was very near being mated. Thomas could see a way out, though. Jürgen wouldn't be able to win, but he could almost force a stalemate. The combination, which involved a queen sacrifice, wouldn't be easy to find but it was there. Thomas closed his eyes and imagined the move Jürgen needed to make next. He tried to will him to do it. But he opened his eyes to see Jürgen reaching for the wrong piece. Wilhelm announced politely, "Checkmate."

"Good game," Jürgen said, collecting all the pieces. He extended his hand to his friend.

"It was," Manfred said. "Very fairly played by both sides."

"Are you surprised?" Thomas asked.

Wilhelm and Jürgen turned to look at Thomas, eyes wide, as if he'd just declared out loud his hatred for Hitler. Thomas knew his heart should have been pounding, his hands clammy. For the second time in a matter of days, he'd spoken back to a Nazi. But he felt calm and fearless.

"By what?" Manfred replied.

"That Jews play fairly. That we aren't all *savage criminals*," he continued, using the exact words from *Der Stürmer.*

The room was silent. The cardplayers stared straight

ahead. The man reading the paper stood up and slipped out the door.

"All I meant was that White was dignified in victory and Black was equally dignified in defeat." Manfred paused. "Let me ask you this . . . had you been playing black, would you have moved differently?"

Thomas jumped at the chance to show Manfred how much he knew about chess. "Instead of moving his bishop, Black should have played queen takes pawn, check, king to rook one, forced, then queen to rook seven, check. Black has to take, and then it's stalemate because the rook pins the bishop." Thomas finished his pronouncement and stared at Manfred.

"I see you know more about chess than shuffleboard," Manfred said, smiling in a way Thomas thought seemed pleased. That wasn't what he wanted at all. He wanted to put Manfred in his place.

"*Guten Tag,*" Manfred said, finally leaving.

It took a few moments for the room to come back to life. Conversations resumed, a man stuffed a pipe, another shuffled the cards.

"Well, well," Wilhelm said, fixing his eyes on Thomas. "You've got a smart mouth, in addition to a talent at chess."

Thomas remembered how Herr Kleist had scolded him that first day they boarded the ship. He didn't care about disgruntling a sour old man like Herr Kleist, but he liked Wilhelm and Jürgen. "I'm sorry. It's only that—"

Wilhelm cut him off. "No apologies. But do be careful. We all want to make it to Cuba, no matter what it takes."

"Of course," Thomas said.

His face felt flushed. He said a polite good-bye and walked out onto the deck. He went to the railing and looked out at the sea. What was down there beneath the boat that he couldn't see? A whole world of fish and sharks and ocean life. He wondered why so many people were willing to put up with the Nazis. Why didn't they fight back? His father had fought back, but only in a calculated way. With secret reports and information. But few dared really fight.

"We need to live to fight," his father had told him time and time again. "Not fight to live."

He understood what his father meant—don't sacrifice long-term goals for short-term desires. It was a theory that was important in chess too. You couldn't just consider your next move; you had to consider the move after that and the move after that. Grand masters were said to be able to think ten moves ahead. Sometimes sacrificing a piece early on would prove worthwhile five moves later. But real life was different from chess, and sometimes Thomas didn't understand how people could just let certain things happen. Like what had happened to his father. How no one—his father, his mother, the people on the street, *he himself*—had done anything. Was that living to fight, or giving up and dying?

Thomas was still in his own thoughts when Günther

ran by. "Thomas! Come on!" He waved to Thomas to join him.

And just like that Thomas was out of his gloomy introspection and running around the deck to the starboard side of the ship. Günther's pockets were bulging, and near the bow something popped out and fell to the floor. Thomas picked it up. It was a bar of soap. From the flowery smell, Thomas guessed it was from the lavatory on the upper deck.

He furrowed his brow. "What's this for?"

"You'll see. We were bored—a case of cabin fever. Just come on!"

Priska and Ingrid waited outside the door to the library.

"What took you so long?" Priska said to Günther.

Günther answered by pulling more bars of soap out of his pockets and giving them to her.

"I've got the water," Priska said, holding up a glass.

Günther dunked a bar of soap in the water. Priska took it from him and slathered it on the door handle.

"What are you doing?" Thomas asked, but Priska put a finger to her lips and shushed him.

"Someone's coming," Ingrid said.

Priska finished soaping the handle and they retreated, hiding behind a nearby lifeboat. Thomas was surprised at how eager she was to pull off the prank. He had never guessed she'd be such a daredevil. It reminded him of the few stories his mother used to tell of her own childhood.

She had also been mischievous, angering her parents to no end, ripping her fancy dresses climbing trees.

Frau Rosen came up to the library door. Today she wore a chic, slim-fitting navy dress over her attractive figure.

Frau Rosen's hand slipped on the doorknob and she wasn't able to turn it.

The group peeked out from behind the lifeboat.

"Mein lieber Gott, was ist das?" Frau Rosen griped, trying again. She shifted the book she carried to under her arm and grabbed the handle, only to have her hand slip again. She grabbed hold once more and yanked. Some of the soapy water must have puddled on the floor because her high-heel sandals slipped and she fell straight onto her backside, cursing. Her dress flew up. Thomas couldn't help but stare, letting his eyes wander from her varnished red toenails to her upper thigh.

Priska was the first to giggle. The giggling was contagious and promptly turned into full-fledged laughter. Thomas wasn't sure if he was laughing from the prank or from his own discomfort with how he couldn't keep his eyes from Frau Rosen's legs.

Frau Rosen scrambled to her feet and headed for the lifeboat. At Priska's lead, they all ran down the stairs. The sound of their feet on the metal slats echoed against the walls. They spilled out onto the tourist-class deck and stood in a cluster, trying to catch their breath between fits of laughter.

"She fell straight on her *Hintern*!" Ingrid said.

Priska held her hand to her mouth as she laughed. Then, stifling her laughter, she said, "I hope she wasn't hurt."

"She was fine," Ingrid said.

Günther whispered to Thomas, his eyes wide, "Did you see her dress come up?"

Thomas nodded.

"Nice legs," Günther said.

Thomas felt Priska's eyes on him, and he sensed she had heard what Günther said.

Priska stood up and walked away from them. Before Thomas could follow and ask her whether she was angry at them, he saw the Nazi officer with the cane approaching. He was scowling and his cane thudded against the deck with each step he took. Thomas rushed forward, hoping to get between him and Priska, but he was too late.

"Do you think this is funny?" the officer demanded of Priska. "Playing tricks?"

Priska hesitated. "A little funny, *sehr geehrter Herr.*"

"As *Ortsgruppenleiter* of this ship, I would like to remind you that while you may feel you have been given a certain freedom, until you are on Cuban soil you are still a subject of the Reich and are therefore accountable to the laws of the Reich and its leader, Adolf Hitler." He wagged a finger in her face. "You are Jews and will be treated as such. Jews do not play tricks."

In Berlin there was an *Ortsgruppenleiter* in charge of

their neighborhood. He enforced the rules and curfews and reported any infractions. Thomas was surprised that the Reich had assigned such a high-ranking Party officer to just one ship. Up close to him now, Thomas noticed he wore a Party badge similar to Manfred's, only the swastika was ringed in not just red but a thick band of gold. Thomas had seen the same badges at home. His father had explained that they were given to the first 100,000 members of the Nazi Party, to reward their loyalty.

With narrowed eyes, the *Ortsgruppenleiter* made sure to stare into the faces of each and every one of them before he clomped away. They walked to the railing, not yet talking. Thomas felt shaky from everything that had happened: the prank, seeing Frau Rosen's legs, being reprimanded by the *Ortsgruppenleiter.*

After a few moments Priska let a laugh escape. She lowered her voice and mimicked, "Do you think this is funny? Playing tricks?"

Günther replied in falsetto, "A little funny, *sehr geehrter Herr.*" Returning to his own voice, he said to Priska, "I liked how you addressed him, very polite."

"Thank you," she said. "And as for you two . . ." She turned from Günther to Thomas, pointing her finger at them. "I saw you looking at Frau Rosen's legs when her dress came up."

Thomas glanced at Günther, who shrugged.

"Don't pretend you weren't."

"It was hard not to," Günther admitted.

"I think she's beautiful too," Priska said.

Thomas wanted to tell Priska that he thought she was much more beautiful than Frau Rosen, but he didn't have the nerve, especially in front of Günther and the others.

"She's so cosmopolitan," Priska added. "Did you know she used to make the ball gowns for the wealthiest women in Prague? All the clothes she wears are her own design."

Thomas smiled, marveling at Priska.

"Did either of you have a girl back home?" Priska asked. Though she had asked them both, Thomas felt her eyes on him.

"Me?" he said. "No."

"There were a few but it feels so long ago now," Günther said casually.

Thomas wasn't sure whether he believed him. Günther asked Priska the question Thomas was eager to know the answer to: "And what about you?"

Priska shook her head. "There was an older boy who lived in our building. He always said he would marry me when I grew up. But then a few years ago he stopped saying that. In fact, he wouldn't even wave to me anymore or say hello if he saw me in the street."

"Because you are a Jew," Thomas said.

Priska nodded a little sadly. "Everything changes so quickly. I didn't really notice that much at first. Marianne and I went to a Jewish school, so we didn't have to leave school like I've heard some others had to. It was *Reichs-kristallnacht* when I really began to understand. The windows of every Jewish store in our town were smashed. All the goods stolen. After that my father said we had to get out. No more waiting for things to blow over."

Günther said, "They took my father that night. They broke down our door, ransacked our apartment, and took my father away—just like that. I thought I'd never see him again."

"What has your father told you about being in a *Konzentrationslager*?" Thomas asked.

At first Günther didn't answer and Thomas worried he'd asked something too private, overstepped boundaries. But he desperately wanted to know what the *Konzentrationslager* was like. They heard rumors all the time but it was impossible to know what was really true.

"They made them work, building something—my father wasn't sure what it even was. They had to carry heavy bags of cement up endless stairs. They were given practically no food and no water, and they were starving and getting sick. My father said it was as if the Nazis were hoping they would die."

They were quiet for a few moments. Thomas wondered if they were waiting for him to say something about his own father. But he didn't want to, and finally Priska said, "Well, enough gloominess. We're the lucky ones. We made it out. Come on, let's go play skittles."

"Good idea," Günther said.

"I don't think I'll come," Thomas said as images of his father bowed down under a bag of cement trampled through his mind.

"Why not?" Priska asked.

Thomas shrugged.

She shook her head and grabbed him by the hand. "You've been taken prisoner. Let's go."

Thomas managed a halfhearted smile and he went with them. But especially after what they had just shared with him, Priska's careless words reverberated in his head. *You've been taken prisoner.* Nothing was innocent anymore, not even a casual, joking remark.

Chapter Seven

Thomas returned to the smoking room often, hoping to find Wilhelm or Jürgen or others playing chess. One day he came in the midafternoon—the time when most people took tea or rested in a deck chair—and the smoking room was near empty. Thomas sat at a table, twiddling his lone pawn through his fingers and imagining it marching down an open board.

"Looking for an opponent?"

Thomas glanced up to see Manfred. "No, just a game to watch."

"How about you and I play?" Manfred asked.

"No thank you," Thomas said immediately.

Manfred frowned. "Do you have other plans?"

"Well, I . . ." Thomas looked around the room. An older man was slumped back asleep in his chair, his mouth gaping open.

"You want to play. I can tell." Manfred leaned closer and said, "What will the other passengers think of you playing one of us?"

Thomas glanced at the swastika on his armband. He knew Manfred meant others would judge him for playing a Nazi, not just a crew member.

"We're all on this ship together . . . might as well make the most of it."

Thomas thought once more of the newspaper clippings he and Priska had seen. So Manfred wanted to play chess with a criminal. Was he that desperate for a partner, or did he just want to prove his racial superiority?

"You're afraid I'll beat you?" Manfred asked.

"No, that's not it at all."

"Then I'll get the board."

As Manfred took the board and pieces out of the cabinet, Thomas knew he could have protested further. But the truth was he yearned for a game. His body tingled as he and Manfred set up the pieces of the simple wooden set.

His father's pieces, including the pawn he carried, were made of ivory. The pieces always felt cool, as if they had been stored in an icebox. The black pieces had been stained and were more brown than black; the white had been left the natural bone color. The pawn he carried was white.

Manfred held out his closed hands to Thomas. Thomas pointed to his right hand. Manfred opened his hand and gave Thomas the black piece. Sometimes Thomas's father claimed he actually preferred to play black. Even though it put a player in a slightly weaker position, he used to say that Black always knew a little more than White. Having to play the second move meant you got a glimpse into your opponent's mind, and then you could react accordingly.

Thinking about his father made Thomas uneasy. The fact that he was here, playing Manfred, made him believe for the first time that his father could actually be dead. He desperately wanted to be in the back room of the print shop, looking at his father across the chessboard. And would his father be disgusted to see him playing a Nazi? Thomas didn't know.

He took a moment to clear his mind, as he liked to do before a game began. Forget everything else—his brother's letter, the other ships, how he found himself hoping to see Priska whenever he went on deck, whether he should even be playing Manfred to begin with—and concentrate on the game.

"Good luck," Manfred said.

"Yes, good luck," Thomas replied. But chess had nothing to do with luck, which was perhaps what Thomas loved most about the game.

Thomas was surprised to find that Manfred disregarded one of the foremost rules of chess: that the center has to be controlled by pawns and that you have to work to support this control. Manfred ignored the center, focusing instead on developing his bishops to long diagonals. After the first few moves, Thomas was confident he'd win. While he took the center with solid pawn pushes, Manfred seemed content to let his pieces merely stare at it from a distance. Thomas followed the lessons he'd learned from his father and from studying the games of the great German chess master Emanuel Lasker. It seemed as if Manfred had never even had a proper chess lesson or bothered to emulate the masters.

Soon Thomas controlled the entire center. He pushed another pawn, grabbing even more space. Manfred moved both his bishops only one square diagonally and then just let them be. "What do you know about Priska?" he asked. His voice startled Thomas.

"What do you mean?" he answered.

"Where's she from?"

"Dresden," Thomas said.

Thomas moved his knight out, twisting it so that its eyes stared across the board at Manfred's king, whose defending knights were sideways.

"Dresden, that makes sense."

"Why?"

Manfred invited Thomas to take the center of the board at will, and Thomas counted on its destroying him later in the game.

"She's very cultured," Manfred said.

Thomas glared at Manfred. "Unlike some other people on this ship?"

Thomas thought how Manfred had a way of saying certain things as if they were casual and harmless, when really they seemed calculated and cruel. Thomas wasn't going to let him get away with it, no matter what the consequences.

Manfred moved his pieces quickly, letting them thump against the wooden surface. Thomas moved his pieces gently, realizing that it was the strength of the move, not the force of it, that won games. He reminded himself to play the board, not Manfred, and so he kept his eyes locked on the black and white squares.

Thomas moved his pawn. Manfred shrugged and then quickly moved his knight to attack the center that Thomas had built. Thomas was sure it would take just a few additional moves before he won; Manfred couldn't possibly survive without pawns in the center. Manfred was breaking every rule except for developing all his pieces.

"It's clear she's from a good family," Manfred said.

"You might be surprised to find that many of us Jews are from good families," Thomas snapped back.

Manfred glanced behind Thomas. *"Guten Tag, Herr Holz,"* he called out.

Thomas turned to see the *Ortsgruppenleiter* raise his arm in salute. *"Heil Hitler!"*

Manfred lowered his eyes and returned a less invigorated *"Heil Hitler."*

The *Ortsgruppenleiter* took one of the sandwiches from the table at the side of the room and lingered nearby. He chewed loudly and it made Thomas feel nauseated.

"Are you on a break?" Holz asked Manfred.

"Yes," he replied.

"Do you usually mix with *passengers* on your break?" He emphasized the word *passengers* as if it pained him to refer to them as such.

"I usually do what I please on my break," Manfred said. "After all, it is my break."

"The captain does not set rules for his steward? About mixing with *passengers*?"

"We're simply playing chess," Manfred said.

"I see that," the *Ortsgruppenleiter* replied.

He stayed awhile longer, methodically eating the sandwich. Finally he saluted again and left. When the door had shut behind him, Manfred sighed.

"You don't like him," Thomas observed. Manfred didn't answer and Thomas added, "Are you going to be in trouble with the captain for playing me?"

Manfred shook his head. "The captain wants us to be welcoming to the passengers."

"I hear we have the captain to thank for being treated so well."

Manfred nodded. "He's a fair man. He has high standards for how he runs his ship, no matter who is traveling on it."

"And the *Ortsgruppenleiter* doesn't agree with him."

"No," Manfred conceded. "*Ortsgruppenleiter* Holz certainly does not."

Thomas was surprised at how forthcoming Manfred was, and he took the opportunity to find out more. "The officers in the Party uniforms . . . are they always on board?"

"No, they were only recently assigned to the ship."

Thomas reached for a knight, about to make a defensive move, when what was happening suddenly hit him—his powerful center was crumbling as Manfred's bishops and knights pressured it into vulnerability. How had he not seen as much? Was it because he was distracted by their discussion? Manfred had seemed as if he didn't know the first thing about chess, but now Thomas realized it might be just the opposite.

Thomas remembered his father telling him about Aron Nimzowitsch, who played very unconventional opening moves that flew in the face of masters like Lasker. He wondered if Manfred knew of Nimzowitsch and Lasker after all. Perhaps Manfred modeled his play after Nimzowitsch and it was all a carefully laid-out plan. Yet Nimzowitsch was a Jew, and it was hard to believe Manfred would aspire to the play of a Jew.

No matter what, it was too late to do anything now, and as Thomas defended, the pressure only grew stronger. Thomas pulled back from the board and closed his eyes. He opened them again, hoping to see things differently, to find a way out. But there in front of him was his disoriented army, and he couldn't get around the fact that there was no point in playing on. He could hardly look up at

Manfred. He tipped his king over. He kept his eyes down for a moment, trying to think through what had just happened. Had there been a method underneath all of Manfred's crazy maneuvers, or had Thomas just let his opponent escape? He wanted to believe the latter, that Manfred really wasn't a good player and that Thomas had just gotten distracted and played beneath his level. He looked up, hoping to see the face of someone buoyed by an unexpected win. Instead he saw the steady gaze of a man who knew just what he was doing.

Chapter Eight

"All they have is war novels," Thomas lamented to Priska.

Boredom had set in again, and they were looking over one of the shelves in the library. Thomas fingered the spines of the books: *Die Gruppe Bosemüller, Aufbruch der Nation, In Stahlgewittern.*

"It looks like someone from the *Reichskulturkammer* has been here," he said.

Thomas kept looking as Priska drifted over to the window.

"Here's one that might be all right—" Thomas said, but Priska cut him off.

"Look," she said, a devilish grin spreading across her face. Thomas came over to the window and saw what she was pointing to—*Ortsgruppenleiter* Holz was fast asleep in one of the deck chairs. Thomas was surprised he had let himself fall asleep in public. He looked almost helpless with his cane lying against his chair.

Priska whispered to Thomas, "I have an idea." Before he could ask what it was, or discuss its merit, Priska was on her way out the door. She snatched Holz's cane and quickly switched it with the cane of an elderly woman who was also sleeping nearby. Both were wooden, but Thomas noted that the woman's cane seemed to be made of a different kind of wood. It was mahogany, whereas Holz's was a lighter color.

Priska motioned for Thomas to follow her. They waited on the other side of a large crate. Priska's face was full of anticipation. When Holz woke, he bolted upright, as if he was ashamed he had fallen asleep. He immediately reached for his cane. The moment his hand was on it, he tensed. So much for playing a trick on him for any length of time, Thomas thought. In that one moment, he had realized it wasn't his cane. He jumped out of his chair, searching the area. He located his cane against the woman's chair and grabbed it. He tucked it under his arm and jabbed her leg with her own cane. *"Aufwachen!"*

She startled awake and looked at him with scared and confused eyes.

He barked, "You had my cane."

"Entschuldige, mein Herr," she said. "I must have gotten confused and taken it by mistake. Please forgive an elderly lady's careless mistake."

He took her cane and threw it at her. It hit her across the chest and she let out a small yelp. She stood up, took the cane, and shuffled off. The *Ortsgruppenleiter* stepped toward her empty chair. Thomas saw him pick up something from the armrest. It was silver and glinted in the sun. He slipped it into his pocket and headed off down the deck.

"Did you see that?" Priska asked, coming out from behind the crate. "What was that he took? A cigarette case?"

Thomas nodded. "I think so."

"I didn't even think he'd notice the cane so fast. He must have been disgusted at the idea of a Jew touching his cane." Priska shook her head. "I feel terrible. I never thought he'd take it out on her, or steal her case."

Thomas furrowed his brow, replaying the scene in his head. It was true that Holz would likely have been disgusted; but then why didn't he automatically wipe the handle clean with a handkerchief?

"How can we get her case back?" Priska said.

"I don't know. I'm not sure we can."

Priska sighed.

"Come on," Thomas said. "I think I found a book."

—❦—

Thomas had never slept very soundly. Back in the apartment in Berlin, there had always been too much going on. He would wake in the wee hours of the morning, listening to snippets of conversation. It was late at night that his parents worked on ways to conceal the information they smuggled out of Germany. They came up with what Thomas thought were ingenious ways to hide papers. They hid them in secret compartments in hairbrushes, mugs of shaving cream, and cigarettes. Once, his father had even designed a way to hide papers in a chessboard. Sometimes when Thomas woke up, his father would hand him what seemed like an everyday object. Thomas's job was to try to find how it opened. If he found it right away, it was not a good-enough hiding place. The next step was making sure the item would fit with the courier's appearance. An unkempt man, for instance, would be unlikely to carry a hairbrush. A man carrying cigarettes should have yellow fingernails. If the item didn't make perfect sense for the person carrying it, it would likely be taken away and the person interrogated.

Once his father went into hiding, there were no more mornings when Thomas found an object to test out. At that point, Thomas was up almost hourly through the night, worrying about his father. And since boarding the ship, he had also woken often, still immersed in dreams of his old life. Even before he would open his eyes, he would smell sweet onions all around him, as if his mother was preparing his favorite meal, *Gulasch.* Or he would see the sun setting over Berlin, like when he and his parents used to take walks, in the years before curfews and the signs saying NO JEWS ALLOWED. They would roam the city, walking by the *Rathaus* and the *Friedrichstadtpassagen* before both were taken over by the Nazis.

On Wednesday morning Thomas was startled awake to find his bunk tilting from side to side. The privacy curtain was swaying. He climbed down from his bunk, did a cursory wash and comb, and went up on deck just as it should have been getting light out, only the sky was dark and cloudy. Between the strong wind and the pitch of the ship, it was hard to walk steadily. Every time he thought that he had found his footing, the deck lurched again, throwing him off balance and nearly to his knees. Nearby, a man had fallen down and a deck boy was helping him up. The wind howled in Thomas's ears. He made it to the railing to see waves crashing against the side of the ship, sending up sprays of water and white foam. Looking out at the swells, he understood for the first time why people referred to the sea during a storm as angry.

After a few moments in the relative safety offered by the railing, Thomas tried to make his way to the dining room. He moved from one solid object to the next, finding stability on a stanchion, a lifeboat, and finally the door to the dining room. He peered inside at the near-empty room. The wooden sides around the tables were up to keep the plates and glasses from sliding to the floor.

He spotted Priska, Marianne, and Professor Affeldt among the few passengers and journeyed across the room to their table. He slid gratefully onto a seat without waiting for an invitation to join them.

"*Guten Morgen,* Thomas. You're not sick?" Priska asked.

"No. Are you?"

"Not yet. My mother's a wreck, though. She's still in the cabin but we couldn't bear it any longer." Priska grimaced and held her nose with her fingers.

A waiter approached, cradling a half-filled cup of coffee. He placed it gingerly in front of Professor Affeldt. Nearby, a few other passengers sipped coffee and nibbled on toast.

Professor Affeldt had dark stubble on his face, but Thomas knew it was better than the cuts he would have endured had he tried to shave. This morning Thomas had been especially grateful that his beard was still light and he only needed to shave every few days. Professor Affeldt motioned to the menus that sat untouched on their table. "Girls, have something light if you want, and then we need to go check on your mother."

"Can't we stay here with Thomas?" Priska asked. "It's so awful in there, Vati."

"Thomas will keep an eye on us," Marianne said, smiling at him. She wore her hair in pigtails, tied with red ribbon.

Thomas remembered what Priska had said about Marianne fancying him. Never having had a younger sibling to look up to him, he found himself enjoying her attention.

Professor Affeldt sighed. "Yes, I suppose. I'm going to try to bring your mother up onto the deck—some say it's better to be up top in the sea air. You can meet us there."

He finished his coffee and got up to check on his wife. Before he left, Priska covered his hand with hers. "We'll meet you on deck soon. We'll give you a break—you must be exhausted."

"Thank you, dear," he said, and smiled proudly at Thomas. "This girl is always looking out for her papa."

Thomas smiled back, but he wondered why Priska was so protective of her father. They watched him walk away, looking like a drunkard as he staggered with the ship's rolling.

Priska ordered plain toast with fruit. Thomas stuck to black coffee. Marianne, despite warnings from both of them, ordered a full breakfast of sausage and eggs.

The food arrived and Priska took a small bite of her toast. The bananas and strawberries slid around on her plate.

The ship came up against a big swell and everything tilted even more. A woman nearby gasped, and then there was the sharp crash of broken glass.

Priska picked at her food while Marianne scraped her plate clean.

"You really are something, Marianne," Thomas said.

She swallowed the last bite and both Priska and Thomas laughed.

"Vati will be up on deck with Mutti soon," Priska said. "We better go help him."

Marianne sighed. "Can't we stay a little longer? What can we do to help?"

"Whatever he needs us to do," Priska scolded her. "Don't be so selfish."

Marianne looked away, and Thomas thought again how protective Priska was of her father.

Thomas walked behind the girls onto the deck. At one point Priska lost her balance and Thomas reached out to steady her. Somehow she ended up almost entirely in his arms, her body for a moment pressed against his. He had his hands on her waist and he was close enough to kiss her. He felt all his blood rushing to a part of his body he generally tried not to think about. Flustered that the thought of kissing her had occurred to him and that his body might betray him, he quickly let go.

She straightened her dress and thanked him. Thomas noticed that her face looked red with embarrassment too. "I'm going to fall right on my *Hintern* like Frau Rosen," she said. "Serves me right!"

He laughed, trying to act as if having her so close hadn't affected him at all, and he hurried up the stairs.

On deck, people slumped in chairs. A few stood clutching the railing. Claudia ran by, her hand pressed to her mouth. Deck boys hurried by with mops and buckets on their way to swab up a mess. The smell of vomit lingered, despite the strong winds.

Frau Affeldt was lying in a deck chair, her eyes closed. Professor Affeldt sat next to her. Thomas noticed the porcelain bowl in Professor Affeldt's hands, and was grateful that it was empty.

"Are you all right, Vati?" Priska asked.

"She's asleep, I think, which is good," he answered. "The doctor gave me some wheat wafers for her when she's able to get them down. He also suggested exercise. Apparently the half of the passengers who aren't up here are in the gymnasium."

The ship lurched. Thomas tried not to look at the water and to ignore the groans of the ship's beams. On the bridge he saw the captain. Manfred was with him and they were surveying the deck, pointing and gesturing to the sick people.

"I'll be right back," Thomas said. He walked over to where the captain was now descending the stairs to the deck. The captain walked steadily, as if his years on the sea had truly given him sea legs. Manfred had disappeared back inside the wheelhouse.

A few moments later, *Ortsgruppenleiter* Holz came out. He was pale and staggered as he walked. Again, Thomas wondered why a landlubber like him would ever be assigned to a ship.

"I just saw the captain's steward," Holz barked at the captain. "He said we're switching directions?"

The captain never took his eyes off the deck. "I can't have my passengers this sick."

The *Ortsgruppenleiter* took a handkerchief from his pocket and pressed it over his mouth and nose. Thomas realized he himself had grown used to the stench. "It's just seasickness. They'll recover. If we change course, we'll lose time."

The captain stood erect; Holz was near to buckling over. "I don't want to slow down either," the captain said, finally turning to look at him. "That's about the only thing we both agree on, but I will not risk my passengers' health either."

Thomas liked the way the captain referred to them as "my" passengers. It seemed fatherly, as if his job was to protect them. But Thomas also told himself that even if for some inexplicable reason the captain wanted to protect them, it didn't necessarily mean he would be able to.

The *Ortsgruppenleiter* narrowed his eyes at the captain. "This will be in my report."

"I have no doubt it will," the captain said.

Holz shook his head and shuffled off. The ship pitched again and he stumbled. Thomas noted that he used his bad leg to steady himself.

"What was that about?" Priska asked, coming up alongside Thomas.

"We're changing course to get out of the worst of the storm."

"That's excellent news," Priska said.

"Except it means we probably won't reach Havana on schedule, which the *Ortsgruppenleiter* didn't like. He doesn't seem to like the captain either."

Even though the captain had returned to the wheelhouse, Thomas was still looking at the bridge, puzzling over the interaction he'd just witnessed. Lost in the intrigue, nearly forgetting that Priska was there next to him, he continued, "I don't trust that man and I'm going to watch him. I'm going to watch everything he does from now on."

"I'll help," Priska said. At her voice, Thomas turned to her. The sea spray had dampened her thick eyelashes and made her curly hair even wilder. Her cheeks were red from the wind. She added, "We'll do it together."

"No, this isn't some prank. This is serious."

"I can be serious," Priska said. "We'll find out what he's doing . . . *together.*"

She was so earnest Thomas could hardly say no. He told himself she was daring and fearless. She was willing to take risks. His mother had always worked in tandem with his father. They talked things through, relying on one another to see what the other might have overlooked.

"All right," Thomas said.

Chapter Nine

Thomas had only been to the pictures once in his life. And he hadn't really enjoyed it.

"How could you have seen only one picture when you live in Berlin!" Priska practically shrieked.

They were standing on deck looking out at the Azores. A halo of morning fog hung over the ship, and the mass of land was just barely visible. Even though the waters had calmed, many people were in their cabins, still recovering from the storm.

"If I had lived in Berlin, I would have seen hundreds of pictures," Priska rattled on. In fact, she had seen fourteen before Jews were no longer permitted in cinemas, and she recounted the title and the plot of each one to Thomas.

"My favorite, favorite, favorite picture is *Mazurka*. It's about a talented opera singer who performs at the Grand Opera House in Warsaw, but she's planning to leave her opera career to marry this rather boring man and become a *Hausfrau*. Then Vera—that's her name—meets a famous composer, Grigorij, and he falls in love with her and tells her she'll never be happy marrying Boris—that's the dull man." Priska talked at a rapid pace and gestured as she continued to explain the plot twists, which Thomas had increasing trouble keeping up with. "She marries Boris, they have a daughter, then he goes off to fight in the World War. She's home with the baby and terribly lonely, so she goes out for a night on the town with her friends and whom should she meet but Grigorij, who is still infatuated with her. Boris comes home wounded from the war, and Vera wants to tell him that Grigorij has been telephoning her and sending letters but nothing romantic has happened between them. Still, she can't bring herself to tell him, so instead she goes to beg Grigorij to leave her alone, once and for all. Boris sees them together and is convinced they are having a romantic affair. He divorces Vera and takes their daughter, Lisa. Vera is left to make a living singing in seedy nightclubs—a woman who once sang at the opera house! Every town she goes to, she searches for her daughter. Then one night her daughter shows up at one of the nightclubs and who is she there with?" Priska paused to raise her eyebrows. "Grigorij! Vera sees Grigorij trying to seduce Lisa, and she pulls out a gun"—here, Priska made an imaginary gun with her hands and aimed—"and bang, shoots him dead. Vera goes to prison for his murder, but it's worth it because she saved her daughter from the fate she herself knew all too well."

Priska closed her eyes and covered her heart with her hands. She started singing, *"Ich liebe dich und du liebst mich. . . ."*

She had a pretty voice and delivered the lyrics, which Thomas assumed must be from the picture, in such a heart-felt manner that he couldn't help but smile. She swayed as she sang, and Thomas loved being able to watch her without feeling self-conscious. When she finished, she said, "Someday you have to see it. You'll fall in love with Pola Negri. She plays Vera. Oh, she's stunning."

"Pictures just seem fake to me, nothing like real life," Thomas explained.

"That's why I love them," she said, shaking her head at him.

Thomas moved the toe of his shoe back and forth along the deck, which was still damp from the early-morning swabbing and the fog. He saw Günther approaching and sighed, wishing he and Priska could have been alone together longer.

"How's your mother?" Günther asked Priska, coming to stand between them.

"She's much better, thank you."

"It was a horrible storm."

Priska looked out at the sea, which was perfectly flat

now. Her face brightened and she pointed. "Look! Windmills! Can you see them?"

"No. . . ." Günther strained to see. "Yes!"

Thomas craned his neck but at first he couldn't make them out.

"There," Priska said, moving closer to show him.

Finally he spotted them, and he felt a tiny rush of connection, more from seeing what Priska and Günther had seen than from seeing the land itself.

"It's easy to forget there's a whole world out there," Günther said. "Sometimes it feels like we'll always be floating on this ship."

"It's because it's hard to imagine what Cuba will be like," Priska said, pushing a stray curl from her face. "We're almost halfway there, you know. Only eight more days." She stared out at the islands and then, as if struck by a sudden thought, turned to Günther. "You're going to the pictures tonight, aren't you?"

"Yes," he said.

She gave Thomas a sidelong glance. "Thomas thinks pictures are silly. Right, Thomas?"

"They just don't seem real." He didn't like how suddenly it was as if Priska and Günther were best friends and he was the odd man out. He wished he had just lied and said the pictures were great.

"Which is exactly the point," Priska countered.

"So you're not going?" Günther asked him.

Thomas thought Günther sounded hopeful. He opened his mouth but Priska answered for him. "Of course he's going."

"Yes," Thomas said. "I wouldn't miss it for the world."

—⁊⁊⁊—

Priska sat between Thomas and Günther. Marianne sat on the other side of Thomas. In the row behind them were Professor Affeldt and Günther's father, whose hair had grown out ragged from where it had been shaved. It stuck up oddly around his skullcap. Thomas tried to picture his own father with a shaved head, but it was hard to do. Frau Affeldt still wasn't feeling well and had skipped dinner too. When Thomas had said, "I thought she was feeling better," Priska had rolled her eyes.

The lights dimmed and the theater quieted. Thomas sat back in the plush velvet seat, telling himself to give the picture a chance. He could feel the energy in the air as everyone awaited the show. He hoped Priska was right and the film could be a welcome escape after all. For two hours they could forget being forced to leave their homes and the uncertain future that lay ahead for them. The projector hummed to life and the image crackled onto the screen. But instead of being transported into a faraway fantasy world, they saw Nazi soldiers on motorbikes and bicycles riding on snowy country roads. The voice-over began: "*After Slovakia declared its independence, the state of*

Czechoslovakia was threatening to crumble. Thankfully, President Hácha put the fate of the Czech State into the hands of the Führer. Despite icy roads and massive snowstorms, the German troops and their Führer marched into Prague according to plan."

People around Thomas gasped. He balled up his fists tightly. The gasps turned to complaints. The grumbling grew louder.

"This is insulting and outrageous!" Frau Rosen called out.

She was close enough to Thomas that he heard her mutter to herself, "Threatening to crumble—the Czech State was doing no such thing. Thanks to France and Britain, he just marched in and took over. Sometime soon a country is going to have the courage to put up a fight, and then there will be war."

The newsreel continued. Motorcars and troops spilled into the city of Prague. Hitler waved from his motorcar and then descended to greet women who smiled and held their hands to their throats as if they couldn't breathe from the excitement of being so near to him. A band played triumphant music in the background. *"Many students and organizations welcomed the Führer. Thousands thanked him for finally bringing Czechoslovakia back home into the Reich, where it belongs."*

Oskar and Elias were sitting down the row from

Thomas. They stood up and moved down the row, bumping against Thomas's knees in their haste. From the row behind, Günther's father put his hands on his son's shoulders.

"Let's go," he said.

Günther stood up. "I'm sorry," he said to Priska.

Thomas's impulse was to leave too, not to stand for being made to watch this. He scolded himself for thinking that two hours of pleasant distraction would even be possible.

Priska turned around to her father, her eyes wide. "Can we stay?"

"Do you want to?"

"I want to see the picture."

Günther squeezed past them with a last regretful look at Priska.

Thomas moved to the front of his seat.

"Are you going to stay?" Priska asked him. "The newsreel will be over soon."

He hesitated, torn between what felt right and what he wanted to do. He wanted to stay with her. He spotted Wilhelm and his wife. They were staying, as were Paul and Claudia. Thomas sat back in his chair but he still felt uneasy.

The picture started. It was an older film starring the great German boxing champion Max Schmeling. He played the role of Max Breuer, an electrician working backstage in a theater in Berlin. When a burly actor made advances toward a young, beautiful aspiring actress, Max came to her rescue, beating the actor up. By virtue of the fight, he was discovered for his talent as a boxer and invited to train at an elite German boxing school.

Thomas watched as Max gave and took blows throughout the picture, but in his head Thomas kept seeing Hitler, his marching troops, and all the adoring people waving handkerchiefs and flags. The only time he could push Hitler from his mind was when he snuck glances at Priska. At the end, when Max won the final match and kissed the young actress, Priska's eyes were half-closed and her face was upturned, as if she were the one being kissed. He closed his own eyes for a moment and remembered how her body had felt against his.

No one in the half-empty theater clapped when the picture ended, and it was silent as they filed out. People moved in front of Thomas and he lost Priska, Professor Affeldt, and Marianne in the crowd. He got stuck behind an elderly woman. He wanted to push around her but he knew it would be rude. He saw Priska again when he reached the door to the hallway, but Professor Affeldt and Marianne were gone. Instead she stood with Manfred.

Thomas stopped short. He heard Priska say, "It wasn't my favorite picture but I did love the final match. It was so exciting. I felt like I was in the ring with Max the whole time."

"Have you seen *Die Nacht der Entscheidung*?" Manfred asked.

"I would have loved to. I adore Pola Negri."

Thomas wanted to tell Manfred what an idiot he was, and how cruel too. Of course Priska would have loved to see that picture, but Jews weren't allowed in cinemas anymore. How could Priska not be offended that he had said that to her?

"She *is* something special, isn't she," Manfred agreed.

Thomas felt sick to his stomach, more so than he had at any time during the storm. He had stayed for her when he should have left, as many others had. And now to see her chatting so easily with Manfred! Did she not have any sense about her? Thomas turned and hurried out the other exit. As he left, he told himself that he was angry because Priska didn't understand the serious nature of their situation. That she treated everything as if it were a game. But he knew it was also because she seemed to actually enjoy Manfred's attention.

—◦◦◦—

He shouldn't have gone on deck that night. But even after what she had done, he still wanted to see her. He played out in his mind what he'd say to her. *Didn't you see the newsreel?* he imagined himself saying. *They played that to show us how things really stand. And then you talk to Manfred like he's a friend?*

It was a foggy night, and Thomas couldn't even see the

water around the ship, let alone a single star in the sky. The wind was strong and he tightened his overcoat around him.

When Priska came on deck, all his practiced words disappeared.

"Where did you go after the picture?" she asked, coming up beside him. "I was waiting for you."

Either she had no idea that he had seen her with Manfred, or she didn't understand what was so wrong with talking to him in the first place.

He said in a clipped tone, "I went out the other way, that's all."

"I waited for you. Vati and Marianne had gone to check on Mutti."

The ship's foghorn blew, and moments later another ship answered far away.

Thomas didn't reply, and Priska said, "Did you like the picture?"

Thomas wouldn't look directly at her as he spoke. "I found it hard to pay attention after the newsreel."

"It wasn't my favorite," Priska continued. "But I did love it when Max knocked out Hawkins in the end, didn't you?"

Thomas offered a barely perceptible shrug.

"Is something wrong?" Priska asked.

Thomas didn't know why he wasn't telling her how he really felt, how upset he was that he had seen her with Manfred. Except maybe it was because that would show her that he cared for her. And perhaps deep down he wished he could be as carefree as she, as blind to everything going on around them.

"Well, if you're not going to talk to me, I'm not going to keep standing here," Priska snapped. "I could get in trouble with my parents if they knew I was sneaking out to meet you."

Her voice was as close to angry as he had ever heard it, and it sent ripples of surprise through Thomas's body. Before he could say anything else, she turned and, with a toss of her curly hair, walked away. *To meet you.* She had said that she snuck out to meet him.

Thomas waited a few moments and then went after her. He was all alone on this voyage, and in the world for that matter, and Priska wanted to be his friend—perhaps even more than a friend. He would be stupid to let her go so easily.

He was reaching for the handle to the door to the stairwell when she pushed it back open. It hit him squarely in the nose. "Ow!"

"Shh!" She grabbed his arm, pulling him inside the passage and down the first few stairs. "Quick."

He followed her, putting one hand to his nose to feel for blood, but it was dry. She stopped a few steps shy of the landing. Voices echoed up the stairwell.

"They can't just decide to make a new law now," someone was saying.

Thomas recognized the voice of *Ortsgruppenleiter* Holz: "Cuba can do whatever they want."

"They can just decide the landing permits are worth nothing and not let them in? Just like that? What are we supposed to do with them?"

Holz said, "We'll drag them back if we have to."

Thomas thought of his own landing permit. His mother had danced him around the kitchen the day she'd secured it. It was one thing to have the money to afford your escape from Germany, and another thing to find a place to escape to. But to Thomas the permit had always seemed like just a piece of paper, and he had never put much faith in paper.

The men's voices faded as they walked away, leaving Priska and Thomas alone on the stairs.

"Are you okay?" She reached out to touch his face. Instinctively he pulled away and then wished he hadn't. He imagined that her hands would have felt cool on his skin.

"It's not bleeding," Priska said.

Thomas touched his nose again. "I think it's fine."

Priska inhaled sharply. "What if they don't let us in? They wouldn't send us back, would they? My family . . . we can't go back."

It was the first time he'd ever heard Priska worry or even acknowledge that things might not work out.

"No one wants to go back," Thomas said, although at

the beginning of the voyage he'd wanted nothing else. But he didn't want to go home as much anymore. Perhaps it had taken being with a ship full of other unwanted souls, each with his or her own painful story, to realize getting out was vital. Or perhaps it was because of Priska.

"Wait until Vati hears—"

Thomas cut her off. "Don't tell him. Not yet. We don't really know anything, and if the whole ship gets talking, then the crew will be more careful about what they say and we won't be able to learn anything more."

"Vati won't tell anyone," Priska assured him.

"Still, it's better not to. Until we know more."

He wanted this to be theirs alone. He wanted them to be like his parents: united in a single cause.

Priska nodded. "All right." She paused and then said, "Why were you being so mean before?"

"I'm sorry," Thomas said. "But you shouldn't be so careless with someone like Manfred."

Priska made a face. "Careless? I was just being nice."

"You shouldn't even speak to him."

Priska rolled her eyes. "What am I supposed to do? Just walk away? That would be rude." She sighed and a funny look came over her face. "Are you jealous?"

"No," Thomas said. "Why would I be jealous?"

Priska shrugged. "No matter what you're feeling, you shouldn't have gotten so mad at me. Friends are supposed to be nice to each other."

"Friends have arguments, though," Thomas pointed out. Priska shook her head. "I hate arguments."

"So you'll just go through life with no arguments?"

"If I can help it."

Thomas laughed. If anyone could go through life without a single argument, he felt sure it would be Priska. As much as he still wanted to be mad at her, he was finding it hard.

"So what next?" she asked. "What about the new law?"

"We keep listening," Thomas said. "Right now that's all we can do."

His voice sounded confident to his own ears, but inside doubts lingered—what if they really weren't allowed in? He also didn't understand why the *Ortsgruppenleiter* would be so cavalier about having to bring them all back. Since he was a Party official, wasn't it his job to make sure Germany had nine hundred fewer Jews?

Chapter Ten

Thomas was not very good at sitting idle, which was how most of the passengers seemed to spend their days. They strolled the deck, read, talked, ate, and played casual games.

Thomas joined Priska, Günther, and the others as they swam in the pool, tried out the mechanical horse in the gymnasium, rode the elevator, and played shuffleboard and Ping-Pong. Whenever he could, Thomas watched people play chess or played himself. That was when time passed most quickly for him, as well as when he was with Priska. As the Affeldts' "cousin," he was allowed to dine in first class with them as he pleased, and he did so regularly. Priska had also invited him to the Shabbos prayer service on Saturday. At first he had been uncomfortable about going. He didn't know the first thing about Shabbos, since his parents had never been practicing Jews. He felt certain he'd make a blunder. And in fact he did—he was late to meet Priska because he'd gone to the social hall, which was where he had heard services took place. After waiting for ten minutes, shifting from foot to foot in his dinner jacket and homburg hat, he had asked a woman if she had seen the Affeldt family.

"Are they Orthodox?"

When Thomas furrowed his brow, she added, "This is the Orthodox minyan. Reform is in the dance hall, Conservative in the gymnasium."

So there were three different levels of faith, Thomas contemplated as he hurried to the dance hall. He had certainly seen the Hasidic men in Berlin, in what Thomas thought was their funny dress and hairstyles, and there were a few people in similar dress aboard the ship. But for some reason it had never occurred to him that people went to different services. He knew that every Jew wasn't strictly religious, but he hadn't known that there was an organized structure.

When he arrived at the door to the dance hall, Priska was not waiting outside. He was now fifteen minutes late and the service was about to start. Either she had given up on him and gone inside, or her family was Conservative. He peeked in and was able to pick out her curly head in one of the back rows. He tiptoed in and sat down next to her. Both she and Marianne were wearing the frilly white dresses he'd first seen them in.

"Where have you been?" Priska whispered to him. She glanced at his head and added, "Oh, good, I meant to tell you to wear a hat."

Thomas surveyed the room and saw that the heads of all the men were covered by either a skullcap or a hat.

"I went to the social hall," he admitted sheepishly.

"You thought we were Orthodox?" she said, stifling a giggle.

"No," he stumbled. "I just didn't really know. . . ."

A man at the front of the room began chanting in what Thomas guessed must be Hebrew. Thomas listened to the rise and fall of his voice—he was surprised to find it soothing even though he had no idea what the words meant. It distracted him in a way that he had hoped the pictures would. He felt an ease he hadn't felt in quite a while. It was the ease he had felt back in Berlin when the apartment was filled with his parents' friends, the hum of their voices. It came from being surrounded by people who shared the same beliefs.

Now the man and a few members of the congregation were preparing to read from what looked like a long piece of parchment wound around two wooden arms.

"That's a tiny Torah," Priska whispered. "Rabbi Zweigenthal brought it aboard in his suitcase. We're lucky to even have a Torah with us on the ship."

Thomas felt proud he knew what the Torah was. He had never actually seen one before, but he had heard about the

Jewish holy book being taken from synagogues and burned during *Reichskristallnacht*. He had heard that each Torah was written by hand and therefore could never be replaced, and that some were hundreds of years old.

After the reading, the man lifted the Torah, wrapped in a velvet cover, and walked around the dance hall with it. When it passed by the row of seats in front of them, Jürgen leaned over and kissed it. When it was their turn, Thomas imitated Priska, who just touched it with her fingertips.

After the Torah was returned to the front of the room, another man, who Thomas assumed must be the rabbi, stood up. Behind him a white sheet had been draped over the large portrait of Hitler. Thomas was glad Hitler wasn't staring down at them, but he wished the portrait had been removed altogether.

The rabbi began, "The celebrated Zionist pioneer Ahad Ha'am, may his memory be blessed, once said that more than the people of Israel have kept Shabbos, Shabbos has kept the people of Israel. As Reform Jews, we no longer consider ourselves bound by the commandments to keep Shabbos as in biblical or Talmudic times—we use electricity, we write, we cook, and sometimes we continue our work. So of what use to us are the words of Ahad Ha'am?"

Thomas looked over at Priska. Her hands were folded in her lap and her eyes were on the rabbi.

"We all know that Shabbos is meant to be a taste of

the world to come, a time to pause and reflect, to be together with loved ones, to be as free of worldly cares as we choose to be, and to commemorate God's rest after the creation of the world. Yet the situation faced by many of us at home has made such a carefree approach intolerable, if not impossible."

Thomas found himself sitting up straighter as the rabbi continued, "Our task on this ship is to remember the blessing as we have celebrated it in the past, and to use the Shabbos of the present as a reminder of the freedom awaiting us in Cuba. We must maintain our hope. This is what this day represents—a beacon of hope in a lost world. When we observe Shabbos, we say that no matter what is happening in the world, the people of Israel will hold fast to their hope."

Some of the women nearby were brushing tears from their eyes. Professor Affeldt took Frau Affeldt's hand. Thomas expected her to share a knowing glance with her husband, confirming the new hope they had for their family. But instead she stiffened.

"And what of our Orthodox and Conservative brethren, also here on this ship? They must find themselves in a predicament—how to observe Shabbos on a moving ship, when using transportation is forbidden to them on this day. Are we to be relieved that our Reform approach permits us uncomplicated Shabbos observance and food consumption? No, my friends, we must not fall into the trap of disunity with our fellow Jews. For in the Talmud we learn that there is nothing that can stand before the duty of saving a life, except the prohibition of murder, idolatry, and incest. Anything is permitted for the purpose of preserving life, even if it means violating Shabbos or eating *treif.* To save a life— *pikuach nefesh*—is the highest principle in Judaism. I only hope our well-learned Orthodox and Conservative friends take this to heart because you all know as well as I that this ship is a giant lifeboat, carrying us all to freedom."

The rabbi paused. The congregation was silent too. Thomas was glad the rabbi felt the same way he did about the voyage—that while it was fun to enjoy the luxuries of the ship and try to forget about what they had left behind, the true nature of their trip would always be with them.

The rabbi continued, "I will end with another statement of the sages of the Talmud, who said, 'Whoever destroys a soul is considered to have destroyed an entire world. And whoever saves a life is considered to have saved an entire world.' Our ship's captain and the Hamburg-America Line are to be blessed for all eternity for the nine hundred lives they are saving with this voyage."

The rabbi sat down. A few moments later the other man began a rousing final song, after which everyone filed out of the dance hall.

Frau Affeldt excused herself, saying she had a headache and needed to lie down.

"What happens now?" Thomas asked Priska.

"Whatever we like," she said.

"You don't have to do more?"

"You really don't understand, do you?" she said. "Shabbos is supposed to be a day of rest, but also a day of pleasure. So after services we enjoy ourselves. What do you want to do today?"

"Should we find Ingrid and Günther and the others?" Thomas actually liked being alone with Priska, but most of the time they did things as a group.

"Günther's Conservative," Priska said. "They'll be there until close to lunch. I still can't believe you thought we were Orthodox." She shook her head. "You knew we didn't keep kosher."

Thomas remembered Professor Affeldt commenting on serving caviar to a ship full of Jews. He also recalled people sending their plates back untouched. "Yes, but I didn't really know who keeps kosher and who doesn't and why not. If you're Orthodox, you can't eat things like caviar?"

Priska shook her head. "Only if it's from the right kind of fish. Fish have to have scales to be kosher. Keeping kosher also means you can't eat pork and you can't have meat and dairy together."

"Why?"

"Because the Torah says so, but people also think some of it might have been for health reasons from a long time ago, before people had modern conveniences like iceboxes—certain foods may not have been safe to eat because they didn't keep as well as others."

"But not all Jews keep kosher?"

"Being Reform means we can be more lenient and do a little bit more of what makes sense in today's world."

Thomas sighed. "I guess I don't know anything about being Jewish." He made a face at how strange that sounded. He was certainly Jewish as far as the Nazis were concerned. "I'd actually like to learn more," he said. "The service was really nice."

While Priska told him some more of what she knew about being Jewish, they wandered around the ship, exploring every corner. They tramped up and down stairs, through passages and across all the decks—from the young children's playroom, with its rubber balls and rocking horse, to the swimming pool, where people calmly breast-stroked back and forth, to the sports deck, where two men played tennis. Priska told Thomas about eating matzo and telling the story of the Jews leaving Egypt during Passover. She explained how once a year they had a chance to reconcile with loved ones and God during the High Holidays, Rosh Hashanah and Yom Kippur. It was a whole other world to him. He didn't blame his father for not teaching him about this part of his heritage, but perhaps for the first time ever he thought about how his life might differ from his parents', in that maybe he would choose to become more religious. Thomas liked listening to Priska. She walked with her head held high, arms swinging, as if the ship were her own private city.

When they came to the door of the lounge, they heard someone playing the piano and voices singing.

Priska's face lit up. "Listen, music!"

Without a moment's hesitation, she threw open the door. Thomas followed. A group of the crew was huddled around the piano, bellowing out lyrics. Manfred and Kurt stood in the middle of them. Thomas shuddered as he recognized the words to the popular Nazi song. *"When Jewish blood spurts from the knife, then it will be twice as good!"*

Priska's face went white. The men noticed her and Thomas. A few stopped singing.

"Enough!" Manfred called.

But some of the men sang louder, even though the man at the piano had lifted his fingers from the keys.

"Don't want to hurt your girlfriend's feelings?" Kurt said to Manfred.

Next to Thomas, Priska stiffened. Manfred stepped away from the piano and moved toward Thomas and Priska, his hands held in front of him, as if about to apologize or explain.

"Don't you know she's just a dirty little Jew?" Kurt said.

Thomas glanced at Priska. Her face was pinched, as if she was about to cry. She looked too old for her frilly dress all of a sudden, like she was wearing Marianne's clothes. Thomas ached for her. He wished the men had chosen to insult him instead. Thomas knew he should take Priska by the hand and leave the room. That was what Herr Kleist and Wilhelm and many of the others on board would have told him to do.

Manfred stood in front of them with Kurt behind him. Thomas's vision blurred with the anger that roiled inside of him. He couldn't see Manfred's features, only the outline of his shape and the splash of color of the gold buttons on his uniform. For that brief moment Thomas actually thought Manfred might stick up for Priska. After all, he did seem to like her. But Manfred said nothing to counter Kurt. And Thomas would not stand by and watch.

Thomas lunged at Manfred, ramming his head into his stomach and tackling him to the ground. He had the benefit of surprise on his side—Manfred hadn't been expecting him to go after him. If anything, he should have gone after Kurt—he was the one who had called Priska a dirty Jew. But he wanted Manfred. Manfred was the one who pretended to be nice and then sang Nazi songs behind their backs. Manfred was the one who liked Priska.

As Thomas fell on top of Manfred, he realized how much bigger and stronger Manfred was. Suddenly he understood how the few years between their ages divided boy from man. They tussled for only moments before the other men pulled them apart. He was surprised the men hadn't let them fight, hadn't cheered Manfred on. But as Kurt held Thomas's arms behind his back, Thomas realized their intent.

"Go ahead, Manfred," Kurt entreated. "Have at him."

"Let him go!" Priska screamed. "I'll tell the captain. You may not like us, but we're your passengers!" Her voice sounded shrill and hysterical.

Thomas stared at Manfred and jutted out his chin. "Go ahead."

Thomas knew he was completely outmanned, but he wanted once and for all to reveal Manfred to Priska for what he really was, no matter the cost of that revelation to himself.

"Let him go," Manfred said to Kurt.

Kurt pulled Thomas's arms tighter. It was easier not to grimace than Thomas thought it would be. His anger dulled the pain.

"I said let him go," Manfred repeated.

Thomas's arms hurt more for a moment after Kurt released him. It must have been the blood circulating back into his limbs. He had been granted his escape but he didn't want it. Kurt stood before him, shaking his head as if he couldn't believe Manfred would pass up a chance to beat a Jew who didn't seem to understand his place in life.

Thomas rushed at Kurt this time, hoping to knock him to the ground. But Kurt withstood the force and came back swinging at Thomas. He hit him squarely in the stomach, sending Thomas sprawling backward onto the floor, the breath knocked out of him. As he struggled to breathe, his stomach burned with pain. But strangely, Thomas didn't mind so much. He found he almost relished the pain. He scrambled to his feet, ready to go back at Kurt, but before he could, Priska grabbed his hand. With one last leer at Kurt, he let her pull him toward the door. On the way out, she bent to pick up Thomas's chess pawn. He hadn't even realized it had fallen from his pocket in the scuffle.

Once on deck with Priska, Thomas made a move toward the door to go back inside and face Kurt again.

"Are you crazy?" Priska yelled. "You're not going in there again." She stepped toward him and said more gently, "Are you all right?"

"I'm fine," he said. He looked down at his stomach, half expecting to see a giant hole in it because of how badly it hurt. He felt a surge of pride—he had acted, he had been courageous.

"You shouldn't have done that," Priska said. "Do you want to get yourself killed?"

"I should have let them say that about you?"

"They were only words."

"I know, and we'll be in Cuba in six days, so just be patient and relax and ignore them, right? Well, I can't ignore them. Sometimes I want to fight back."

Thomas heard his father's voice in his head. *Live to fight. Don't fight to live.* He sighed, his sense of pride dulling. His father would have wanted him to walk away.

Priska held out the pawn to him. "You lost this."

He nodded and took it from her. "It was my father's."

She asked, "Were you at home when he was taken away?"

Thomas swallowed. He had never told anyone what had happened, but he knew that in a way he had been waiting for the right person to tell. He turned the pawn over in his hand as he spoke. "My parents decided a few nights after *Reichskristallnacht* that the safest thing to do was to temporarily split up. It was too dangerous for my father to stay with us. He knew that without him we would have a better chance of survival. They decided my father would go live with a cousin a few towns over, where he could hide. I hated that he had to go but I also understood why."

Priska's eyes were focused on Thomas as he talked. Every time he felt himself faltering, he traced the pawn's edges.

"After he left, we got letters from him every so often and we wrote back. The letters had to go through a friend of a friend. Then one day—it had been three months since he left—my mother and I were in town doing the shopping. On the way home we walked by the train station, where three Nazis were beating a man. Usually we would have kept on walking. You don't stick your nose where it doesn't belong unless you want trouble. Perhaps it was because we hadn't gotten a letter from him in two weeks, perhaps my mother just sensed something in the air. She walked closer and I followed. The man was on the ground. He struggled to sit up and blood spurted from his nose and mouth. He didn't try to stop it, and I saw that one of his arms was hanging by his side. It must have been badly broken. It was at a crooked angle; it looked like it didn't even belong to his body anymore. I finally looked closely at the man's face. Even through all the blood . . ."

Thomas stopped and looked away. His fist was clenched tight around the pawn, forcing its sharp edges into his skin.

Priska made a small sound. Before she could say anything, Thomas kept going. "The Nazis saw us. 'Do you wish to see a Jew die?' one of them asked. My mother shook her head. She took my hand and held it very tightly, as if she was telling me not to move, not to say a word. The Nazi must have seen something in her face, or in the way we were holding hands. We hadn't said anything or even looked at my father as if we knew him. I could tell from his eyes he recognized us, of course. But he was too smart to let on.

" 'Do you know this man?' the Nazi asked us. His voice was softer. He wanted us to admit to knowing him; he wanted us to fall into his trap. If we admitted to knowing him, we might all die."

Thomas took a deep breath. His throat felt scratchy. "My mother didn't say anything. She just shook her head, turned, and, pulling me with her, walked away. That was the last time we saw him." Thomas unclenched his fist. His skin had red grooves where he had gripped the pawn. He thought Priska would say something optimistic, as she always did. Always trying to look on the bright side so much that it could drive you crazy. It was what was charming about her, and also what was frustrating.

But this time she shook her head and said, "Oh, Thomas. I'm so sorry."

"Now do you understand why you can't trust someone like Manfred?" Thomas asked her. He meant after what had happened before, with the song and the insults. But maybe he also meant after what he'd just told her.

"Yes, I do."

Thomas closed his hand around the pawn again, this time more lightly.

"And the chess piece?" Priska said. "The pawn. Not a king or queen."

"The pawn is the most misunderstood, underestimated piece in the game. It is the foot soldier, yes, but it has the most power. It creates the structure and the order of the game. The French chess player François-André Philidor once said that 'the pawn is the soul of chess.' "

When he had boarded the ship and met Priska for the first time, he never imagined that she would be the one he would tell his secrets to, but now that he had started, he wanted to confess everything. "My parents were part of the resistance. That's why my father got taken away, I'm sure of it—that and, of course, because he was a Jew, and a Jew married to a non-Jew, no less. I always wondered why my parents and their friends didn't do more, like set bombs or fight back. But when I asked him, my father said you need to live to fight, not fight to live."

"What does that mean exactly?" Priska asked.

"It means we have to bide our time, be careful, and then we will be able to make a difference in the fight."

"And do you agree with him?"

"I don't know," Thomas said, lowering his eyes. "What did it get him?"

Chapter Eleven

The next day, Wilhelm asked Thomas to play chess. After the fight with Manfred and Kurt and telling Priska about what had happened to his father, Thomas welcomed the distraction.

"Where's Jürgen today?" Thomas said as they set up the pieces.

"He's still feeling the aftereffects of the rough seas," Wilhelm explained. "Back when we fought in the World War, Jürgen suffered heavy injuries. He was lucky he lived, in fact. If he gets sick now, it hits him hard."

Thomas straightened his last piece. With every small movement he made, he felt it in his stomach, which he'd found that morning was black-and-blue. Thomas still didn't mind the pain, though. Sometimes he moved even if he didn't have to, just to make sure the pain was still there. "You both fought in the World War?"

"Together, in the same battalion. Hard to imagine Jews fighting for Germany these days, isn't it?" Wilhelm shook his head. He raised his finger. "Of all the laws, do you know which one made me the most enraged? The law that forbade me from flying the German flag. I risk my life for Germany and then I'm forbidden from flying a German flag outside my home? That's when I knew it was time to get out. Other people kept hoping things would get better. But when you turn your back on people who risked their life for your country, then you have lost your senses. And the latest news . . . you've heard, I assume?"

Thomas shook his head. He picked up a pawn in each hand—black in his left, white in his right.

"Hitler and Mussolini have signed a pact. If there's war, they've sworn to support each other."

Wilhelm won the chance to open and began with a straightforward pawn-to-queen-four opening. After the first few moves, Thomas breathed a sigh and felt his whole body relax. Unlike Manfred, Wilhelm played according to the classical rules. Thomas knew that he was, in essence, staying in his range of comfort to play Wilhelm, but his game against Manfred had left him off-kilter. For now he decided it was just fine to rebuild his confidence.

By his eighth move, Thomas had accomplished many of his opening goals—he had gotten his king to safety, moved out his bishops and knights, and controlled a good bit of the center. Thomas sat back, pleased with himself. He was playing intelligently and he was a solid rival for Wilhelm.

Wilhelm cupped his hand around his chin and looked at the board before making his next move. Thomas could tell he was scanning variation upon variation. He moved a pawn. A mistake, Thomas thought; now he has nowhere to hide. Thomas slid his rook down a file and announced, "Check." Wilhelm's king stood squares away from refuge. Wilhelm shifted in his seat. Thomas could feel the momentum tipping solidly to his side. He had expected to feel satisfied that the game was going his way and he was outplaying Wilhelm. But the game with Manfred still rattled through his mind. He tried to tell himself that he had just played poorly that day and if he were to play Manfred again, things would be different. He wouldn't let Manfred distract him with talk. But deep down Thomas knew that wasn't why he had lost to Manfred. Thomas was on solid footing against a player like Wilhelm, but an unconventional player like Manfred threw him off balance.

Wilhelm cleared his throat. It was Thomas's move. Every one of his pieces had long open files and diagonals due to fearless attacking over the last few moves. All he had to do now was make two more moves and he would win Wilhelm's queen. Thomas moved a piece and continued going about the last remaining work to be done, still surprised that beating Wilhelm wasn't that satisfying. Wilhelm wasn't whom he wanted to beat.

"Good game," Wilhelm said. "Someone has taught you very well."

"My father," Thomas said.

"I've noticed he's not on the ship with you?" Wilhelm made his statement into a question to be polite, Thomas thought.

"No. He was taken to Dachau."

"I'm sorry," Wilhelm said.

Thomas felt heat gathering behind his eyes. If his father were here, he could ask him how to play Manfred. Without his father, he had no one to turn to. And there was so much more he needed his father for than chess. Thomas succeeded in pushing away any tears. He checked to see if Wilhelm had noticed his pain. Wilhelm was looking at him with kind eyes, and Thomas asked, "Have you ever played someone who doesn't look to control the center?"

"A player like Nimzowitsch?"

Thomas brightened. "Exactly."

Wilhelm clucked. "Not really."

"Well, if you were to, how would you play him?"

"One would be tempted to succumb to his type of game, but you would need to stick to what you know best. You need to respect his way of playing, yes, but be even more confident in your own." Wilhelm started to clean up the board.

Thomas motioned for him to leave the pieces. "I'm going to practice." He reached across the board for the black pieces but stopped and gritted his teeth against the pain in his stomach.

"Are you all right?" Wilhelm asked.

"Fine," Thomas managed.

"Oh, really?"

Thomas closed his eyes while the wave of pain passed. He opened them to find Wilhelm still looking at him.

"Stomachache?" he said, raising his eyebrows. "Or did your smart tongue get you into trouble?"

"Maybe," Thomas admitted.

Wilhelm smiled. "You're young. You're bound to be headstrong. But be careful. Be smart."

Thomas nodded.

The door opened and Priska breezed in. "Thomas, there you are."

Thomas looked up and smiled. If anything, he felt that what had happened with Kurt and Manfred had brought them closer.

Priska looked at Wilhelm. "I'm sorry . . . am I interrupting?"

"No, we just finished up."

"Who won?" she asked.

Wilhelm put on his hat and started for the door. He said with a smile, "He put an old man in his place."

The door closed behind Wilhelm, and Priska scooted into his vacated seat.

"How's your stomach? Does it hurt?"

"A little."

Priska sighed. Before she could tell him once again how stupid he had been, he said, "Want to play?"

"I don't know how. You'd have to teach me."

"I've never taught anyone before." Thomas had always been the student, and he wasn't certain he was comfortable with the roles reversed.

She said, "I'm sure you'd be a great teacher."

"No one ever taught you to play? Not your father?"

"My grandfather tried to but I was too busy with friends and school."

"Did your grandfather stay behind in Dresden?"

"No, he died, a year ago now, I guess it is."

"I'm sorry," Thomas said.

"We wouldn't have been able to leave if he hadn't died. He was too sick to travel and my mother wouldn't leave without him. If it hadn't been for him, my father would have had us out a long time ago. With my grandfather gone, my mother was out of excuses."

Priska picked up a knight. "I remember that each piece moves differently but I can't remember the particulars. Teach me?"

"Now?"

"What else do we have to do that's so important?"

He nodded, acknowledging that she had a point. Sometimes time felt endless on the ship. He picked up the pawn. "Pawns can move forward but can only capture diagonally. The pawn can move two steps on the first move but only one step at a time for the rest of the moves."

Priska nodded.

"There's one other thing about the pawn," Thomas continued. "When the pawn reaches the end of the board, it can change into any piece you want except for a king. The pawn is the least valuable piece, so if you trade it for something, you'll be in better shape."

"Do most pawns get to the end of the board?"

"Most don't make it. But the ones that do are more valuable than any of the other pieces."

Next Thomas picked up a knight. He moved it along the board to demonstrate as he explained, "The knight moves in an 'L' shape, either two squares up or down and one square to either side, or two squares sideways, one square up or down. The knight can also jump over pieces. My father taught me that the way to remember that is because the knight is a horse—that's why it can jump over the other pieces."

Thomas went on to explain how the bishop, rook, queen, and king moved. He wasn't sure Priska was really paying attention, but he liked being there with her nonetheless, so he kept going. When he finished, he said, "All right. Do you remember how the bishop moves?"

Priska smoothed back a piece of her hair. "Not really."

"Diagonally, as many squares as it wants."

"I remember how the knight moves." She picked one up

from the board. "I like the knight because it doesn't move anything like the other pieces. These other ones keep getting in each other's way, and I like how the knight can just move past its obstacles effortlessly."

Thomas shook his head and smiled. It was just like Priska to personify a chess piece.

Before Thomas could quiz Priska on how the rook moved, she said, "Only four more days until we're there. Can you believe it? It seems like we've been talking about leaving and waiting since forever. What's the first thing you'll do in Havana? I'll have a pineapple. I've never had a real pineapple, straight from the tree."

"I'll telegram my mother," Thomas replied. If he had had enough money, he would have telegrammed her already, as others had done for their families. He would have let her know that the journey was almost over and that he was safe. That was all she wanted—to see him safe. "Can you imagine living in a place where we can walk around without curfews?"

Priska grinned. "We can go to the pictures again! I'm going to go right after I have my pineapple."

"They'll be in Spanish," Thomas pointed out to her. "You won't understand a thing."

"Oh, I don't care." Priska put the knight back on the board. She straightened it so it sat right in the middle of the square she had placed it on. "Did you hear about the big party? It's customary on ocean liners two nights before docking. It's going to be a costume ball." Priska's face lit up as she continued. "I wonder what people will dress up as. My mother said we could go to the beauty salon and get our hair done again. The first thing we did when we came aboard was to get our hair done. Of course, we haven't been allowed in beauty salons for years. Back in Dresden a woman in our neighborhood who used to have her own shop did hair in her home, but it's not quite the same as walking out of a salon with your hair just perfect." Priska sighed. "Although it doesn't matter how perfect my hair is because I'm not allowed at the ball—only grown-ups."

Thomas looked at the board. "Do you want me to explain checkmate?"

Priska shrugged. "I think maybe I learned enough today. Just trying to keep the pieces straight is a lot. You can teach me more some other time."

"All right," Thomas said, although he was pretty sure she didn't have the patience for chess.

Thomas returned the chess set. They went outside and walked around the deck. A lone gull flew overhead, and Thomas wondered where the bird had come from and where it was going. The gull swooped down closer and then, as if disinterested in what it had seen on deck, soared back to the sky.

Thomas saw Manfred walking toward them. He didn't know whether he should warn Priska, and then it was already too late and Manfred was passing them. Thomas made certain to meet Manfred's eyes, to try to tell him with a single look that he must never bother Priska again and that Thomas was not scared of him. That at any moment he was ready to finish what they had started. Thomas put his arm around Priska, as he'd seen Paul do with Claudia.

Priska held on to his other arm tightly, and Thomas felt her steer him away from Manfred. "Only four more days and we'll never see him again," she said.

Chapter Twelve

Since the pool had been put up, they had swum at least once a day. The weather became milder the farther south they traveled. The bruise on Thomas's stomach had faded to a faint yellow, but Thomas still dove right in so that no one would notice. Günther jumped in too, sending up a giant splash that soaked Priska and the benches that lined the pool.

"You're all wet now, so you might as well come in," Günther called to her.

Priska made a face at him and slid in.

The pool was small, perhaps the size of the sitting room in the apartment in Berlin, and Thomas only had to swim a few strokes to reach Priska. She wore a bathing cap and Thomas missed seeing her curly hair.

Priska splashed Thomas and he splashed her back. A few of the others joined in, and they had a splashing fight until Marianne got water up her nose. Then Priska suggested they dive for coins. Ingrid went to fetch some coins from her mother, who sat nearby reading a book in the shade of a striped umbrella. Thomas and Priska treaded water next to each other.

"Don't splash again," Priska said.

"I won't," he promised.

Ingrid reappeared with a handful of coins.

As they swam to the side and pulled themselves out of the water, Thomas whispered to Priska, "I've been thinking more about the *Ortsgruppenleiter*'s cane." He had been thinking about everything they knew about Holz, going over all the facts. He used a cane but had only a minor limp. His cane was very important to him. He detested Jews and was a Nazi official but didn't seem to care if they had to take the whole ship of them back to Germany. He was a thief.

Priska climbed out of the pool. She wore a red two-piece bathing suit and Thomas could see the real shape of her body. She had a small waist that made him want to put his hands around it. He could also clearly make out the curves of her breasts. He looked away, not wanting his own body to embarrass him in front of everyone.

"Who's diving first?" he asked.

"Let's go by age," Priska suggested.

"That means I'm first," Günther pointed out.

"I'll throw," Thomas said. He tossed in a coin, which landed with a plink.

Günther dove in and promptly resurfaced. "That was too easy."

Soon they were up to tossing four coins. On Thomas's turn he picked the first three coins off the bottom easily but couldn't find the fourth. His chest ached but he forced himself to keep looking. Finally, at just the moment he couldn't stand it any longer, he saw it. He made one last kick, grabbed the coin, and burst out of the surface, gasping for breath. He climbed out of the pool and stood with his arms folded over his stomach.

Günther threw four coins in for Priska. She dove in neatly, barely making a splash, and was promptly back up with the coins, hardly even out of breath.

"Well done," Günther said.

Thomas saw Günther's eyes on her, much as his own had been. Thomas motioned to where Ingrid stood, poised to dive. "Günther! Ingrid's ready."

As Günther tossed coins for Ingrid, Priska came to stand next to Thomas. "What have you been thinking?"

"We need to have a look at the cane."

"What for?"

"Maybe there's a secret compartment and he's hiding something in it."

Priska's eyes widened. "Like what?"

"Gold. Diamonds. We already know he's a thief.

Maybe he's hiding valuables he's stolen from other Jews. He's going to sell them and either keep the money for himself or, more likely, give it to the Reich."

Günther threw coins for Jakob and then for Marianne. She emerged from the pool holding her coins triumphantly. "Thomas!" she shouted. "I got all of them!"

"Bravo!" Thomas said to her. Then, lowering his voice, he said to Priska, "The question is how will we ever get our hands on it?"

"Hmm," Priska said. "It won't be easy, especially if you consider how mad it made him when he thought that old lady had it."

"Priska," Günther called, holding out the coins to her. "Will you throw for me? Make it really difficult."

"All right," she said.

She scattered them at opposite sides of the pool. Günther was under the water awhile. Thomas hoped he wouldn't be able to get them all, since it was clear he was trying to impress her. But he came up smiling. "Got 'em. You need to make it even more difficult next time. Your turn, Thomas."

Priska scattered the coins again, as she had for Günther. Thomas took a huge breath and dove in. Again, he found the first three but couldn't find the fourth. His insides felt as if they were caving in on each other, yet he kept looking, sweeping the bottom of the pool with his hand. When he couldn't hold his breath any longer, he had to come up.

"Almost," Günther said.

Just as Priska was about to take her turn, the lifeguard announced that adult swim was starting. The group issued a collective moan. Thomas and Priska went to fetch their towels. Thomas pulled the towel around him, covering his stomach. Now that he was out of the water, the air gave him gooseflesh. He noticed that Priska's fingers were wrinkled.

A few of the adults had meandered in and were wading into the pool for their daily constitutional, much like the ones who walked the circumference of the ship each morning after breakfast. Günther ran back to the pool and cannonballed in, sending water flying over the edge of the pool. The adults shrieked and the lifeguard berated Günther. Thomas was certain Günther had done it for Priska's benefit, and it did have an effect on her, just not the one Günther had been hoping for.

A sly smile came over Priska's face. She said to Thomas, "I think I know how we can get the cane."

———◦∾◦———

Priska promised Thomas her plan would work. In the late afternoon many of the passengers rested in deck chairs on the middle deck, where the wind was not so strong, closing their eyes and often falling asleep. Priska armed Marianne, Jakob, and Hannelore with long pieces of string, and they dangled their strings over the railing, across the faces of the people below. When the adults showed signs of annoyance—an opening eye, a batting hand—the kids pulled the strings up, waited, and then let them down again. With the game well under way, Priska ran to alert Thomas, who had been keeping track of where the *Ortsgruppenleiter* was. Thomas rushed up to him and said, "*Mein Herr,* some of the kids . . . they're bothering the passengers again!"

Holz scowled. "Where are they?"

"I'll show you but you better hurry."

He followed Thomas to the middle deck. Thomas walked quickly, testing to see if his bad leg would slow him down, but he kept up with him. Thomas was certain his hunch about Holz was correct. Thomas pointed up to where Marianne, Jakob, and Hannelore stood overhead, giggling and dancing their strings across the faces of the people below. A few of the passengers were standing now and scolding them. The *Ortsgruppenleiter* narrowed his eyes and demanded, "Come down here at once!"

Marianne, Jakob, and Hannelore turned and ran. At just the moment Holz was about to give chase, Priska darted out from behind a deck chair. Thomas had faded back behind one of the lifeboats, and he watched as Priska reached for the cane. She grabbed it and ran off, calling, "Try to catch them now!"

"Come back here!" the *Ortsgruppenleiter* barked after her.

Thomas was convinced that Holz could walk just fine without the cane, but he assumed the man didn't want to reveal as much. Priska circled around the whole deck in order to lose the *Ortsgruppenleiter.* She came back over to Thomas, jumped into the lifeboat, and handed him the cane. He ran his hand down the wood from top to bottom, feeling for grooves. At the same time he searched with his eyes for imperfections in the grain of the wood.

"Hurry!" Priska said. "We don't have much time."

She leaned partly out of the lifeboat, searching for the *Ortsgruppenleiter.*

"Do you see him?" Thomas asked.

"Not yet, but hurry. You only have a few minutes, at most."

With his father's tests, Thomas had never had a time limit. His face grew hot as he found nothing out of the ordinary. He had been so sure that Holz was a thief and that the cane would have a secret compartment.

"He's coming!" Priska cried.

Thomas grabbed the cane by the handle and, cursing under his breath, knocked it hard against the bottom of the lifeboat. He paused, cocking his head to one side, then repeated the action. The sound wasn't right. It didn't make enough noise for the force with which he had slammed it against the lifeboat. Not the amount of noise a solid wooden cane should make.

Before he could try it a third time, Priska reached for the cane. "Quick!"

Thomas reluctantly gave her back the cane. She popped out, assuming a charmingly contrite smile.

"Here's your cane, *Mein Herr.* We were just having a little fun."

The *Ortsgruppenleiter* seized the cane and leaned close, sticking his finger in her face. "Listen to me, you snotty Jew girl. Next time I'll throw you overboard, and you'll be torn up by the engine into tiny little Jew pieces that even the sharks won't want to eat." He leaned closer so his big face was eye to eye with hers before he hulked away.

Thomas climbed out of the lifeboat, his heart charging in his chest. He was on his way after Holz when Priska stepped in front of him.

"Just words, remember?"

Thomas wanted to run after him and knock him down for what he'd said to her. But it wouldn't get him anywhere. *Live to fight,* he thought. *Be careful, be smart.* He had to find out more about the cane and what the *Ortsgruppenleiter* was up to. He took a deep breath.

"It's hollow inside. I'm sure of it. If we could get our hands on it for longer . . . I could figure out how to open it."

"There's no way he's going to let it out of his sight now."

"No," Thomas said. They had been so close.

"So where does that leave us?"

Thomas sighed. "Still monitoring him. Even more closely now."

—✐✐✐—

That night Priska didn't come up on deck. Thomas felt their night watch was more important than ever. They needed to listen for news about the other ships and the validity of the landing permits, as well as anything more they could find out about the *Ortsgruppenleiter*. Thomas waited for her past midnight, when the deck lights were turned off, before he finally decided to go to her cabin. He hadn't planned what to do when he got there, and he stood outside for a few moments considering options. If he knocked, he might wake Marianne. He could slip a note under the door, but he would have to go fetch paper and pen. He moved closer and put his ear to the door. Nothing. He moved back, feeling foolish, when he heard sobbing. It was coming from Priska's parents' cabin. Was she in there? he wondered. Had something happened and that was why she hadn't been able to meet him? Had Manfred or Kurt bothered her again?

Thomas heard Professor Affeldt's voice: "You can't just cry like this for hours. You need to stop crying and stop having headaches and start being part of this family. We need you. The girls need you."

Thomas stepped closer to the door.

"I can't," Frau Affeldt said. "It isn't that easy for me. I—"

Professor Affeldt cut her off. "We're on a ship headed to Cuba. In three days we'll be starting a new life."

From inside the cabin came what sounded like the

pound of fist against door. Thomas jumped backward, his heart leaping. Professor Affeldt said something else, but Thomas couldn't make it out over the rushing blood in his ears. The door opened, and it was too late for Thomas to run down the passage and escape being seen. He was face to face with Professor Affeldt, who startled at seeing him.

"Thomas? Is everything all right?"

"Ah, yes." Thomas tried to gather himself and think of excuses for why he was there. "Yes, everything's fine."

"Was there something you needed? The girls are asleep. It's late—you should be asleep too."

"I just . . . I overheard something . . . the crew was talking about our passes not being valid." It was the only thing Thomas could think of that would be a good-enough explanation for his presence. Also, the closer they got to shore, the more he really did wonder whether they would be admitted.

Thomas expected Professor Affeldt to be surprised, but he nodded. "You know about this?" Thomas asked.

"Yes, I've heard something about it."

"Is it true?"

Professor Affeldt looked straight at Thomas as if he was gauging whether he could be honest with him. "You're a smart young man, Thomas. And clearly you are smart enough to know rumors often have some truth to them." Professor Affeldt reached out and placed his hand on Thomas's shoulder. "You're a good friend to my girls, and

I'm pleased you're spending time with our family. They need a friend, especially Priska. She may seem sure of herself but underneath she's still a young girl. I've always tried to protect her and Marianne, and sometimes I think I've protected them too much."

Thomas thought about how hard Priska tried to protect her father. In fact, they were both trying to protect each other. Thomas assumed that Professor Affeldt meant he had protected them from the many bad things the Nazis did, but he added, "Frau Affeldt and I . . . well, we don't always see things the same way." Professor Affeldt paused. "It's nice to know there's another person looking out for my daughter. Thank you for that. And for the girls' sake, let's keep what we've talked about tonight between us."

Thomas nodded, although Priska already knew the rumor about the passes. Thomas wondered if Priska knew anything else that her father thought she didn't. He thought about how Frau Affeldt never ate and looked so detached most of the time. Upon first glance when he had boarded the ship, he had thought the Affeldts were the perfect family. Priska often acted as if they were. But now he wondered if much of her attitude was a charade.

"Was there anything else, Thomas?"

Thomas shook his head.

"Then go to bed. We all need our sleep."

Chapter Thirteen

The next day Priska apologized for not meeting Thomas. "I don't know what happened," she said. "I must have just fallen dead asleep."

Thomas didn't question her. For her sake, he hoped she *had* been asleep and had slept right through her parents' row.

That day Thomas went to the purser's office to pick up his landing card. But while everyone else took theirs with a broad smile, Thomas remained stoic. He was still not quite ready to believe that the passes were the key to freedom. The two other ships and the possible revoking of the passes loomed in his head, not to mention the strange behavior of the *Ortsgruppenleiter.*

Later that night the crew transformed the social hall from synagogue to ballroom. The tables and wicker chairs were pushed to the sides to create a dance floor, and balloons and streamers hung from the second-floor balcony.

Thomas didn't care that they were not invited to the costume ball, but Priska had begged her parents to at least let her watch the partygoers make their entrances down the grand staircase. Priska, Marianne, Günther, and Thomas stood in the wings of the balcony as everyone arrived. As promised, Priska had gotten her hair done at the beauty salon. Her wild curls had been straightened. Priska was proud of her new look, but Thomas preferred her hair the way it usually was.

"Look at Herr Bruhl!" Priska said, pointing.

Thomas smiled. There was something to be said for the passengers' ingenuity and resourcefulness. With a bedsheet for a gown and a towel wrapped around his head, Herr Bruhl was dressed as an Arab sheik.

The arrival of Paul and Claudia sent all four of them into fits of laughter. Paul wore Claudia's dress and high heels. He had her necklace on and her lipstick too. She wore Paul's coat and tie and had slicked her hair back and drawn on a mustache.

Lisbeth had made herself up as a clown with Margot's tiny hat perched cockeyed on her head, a bow from one of Margot's dresses pinned on her chest, a big red mouth painted on her lips, and red dots on her cheeks.

"And there's Vati," Priska said, bringing her hand to cover her heart. "Doesn't he look dashing? I helped him with the makeup."

Professor Affeldt was dressed as a pirate with a scarf tied around his head and a sash around his waist.

"What's your mother supposed to be?" Günther asked as Frau Affeldt took her husband's outstretched hand to walk down the stairs. She wore a regular evening gown.

"She said she didn't feel like dressing up," Priska replied, her voice quiet. Priska pointed to Frau Rosen. "If I got to dress up, I'd be a geisha girl. She looks beautiful, doesn't she?"

"I'd be a pirate like your father," Günther said.

"What about you, Thomas?" Priska asked.

"I don't know."

"Oh, come on. Don't be so dull."

Thomas scanned the crowd. Günther's father had come as an Olympic athlete. The shirt and shorts revealed how skinny he still was from being in Sachsenhausen. Günther's father was one of the only reminders for Thomas that this wasn't a normal shipboard costume affair. The other was the stern gaze of Hitler staring down from the portrait, which had been uncovered again since the services.

"Marianne and I would wear each other's clothes, like Paul and Claudia," Thomas said.

Marianne's face lit up. "That would be so much fun."

The people below danced, talked, kissed, and raised champagne flutes in exuberant toasts. Thomas enjoyed watching. But no one loved it more than Priska. She hummed along with the music, sometimes shuffling her feet or swaying in time, entirely enchanted.

At ten o'clock, Professor Affeldt came up to the balcony and told Priska and Marianne it was time to go to bed.

"You look very handsome!" Priska said.

"Thank you, my dear," he replied. He took her by the hand and spun her around in a little dance.

She giggled. "Are you having fun? You should ask Mutti to dance. You haven't danced once."

Thomas searched out Frau Affeldt. She was at the bar having a drink. Thomas willed Priska not to look for her mother so she wouldn't find her there.

"Do I need to go with you to the cabin to make sure you go to sleep?" Professor Affeldt asked.

"No, Vati, but you really must dance with Mutti."

"Yes, yes, I will."

"Promise?"

Professor Affeldt nodded. Priska kissed him good night and the four of them left the ballroom. Outside, the deck seemed strangely quiet. The lights glimmered on the sea.

Priska whispered to Thomas and Günther, "I'll meet you back up here in half an hour!"

Before either could answer, she and Marianne trotted off, hands linked.

Priska came back, as promised. The music had changed from Glenn Miller to rumbas and tangos. They snuck back in and watched men and women dancing cheek to cheek. Thomas spotted Frau Affeldt still at the bar. He saw Priska search the crowd for her, and he hoped again that she wouldn't be able to find her. But she did, and her face fell. After a few moments she said to them, "Let's go back outside and dance."

Outside, Priska held out a hand to each of them. She called out too loudly, "Who will tango with me?"

Thomas hesitated. The only person he had ever danced with was his mother.

Günther stepped forward, and Thomas cursed himself for being slow and reluctant. "Madame," Günther said, reaching to take her hand.

As Thomas watched, he became more angry with himself. From the looks of it, Günther was not an expert dancer either, but it hadn't stopped him.

"Straighten your back," Priska instructed Günther. "Look this way. Your face closer to mine. Now go—"

And off they went, jerking down the deck. Thomas laughed loudly so they would hear him and remember they weren't alone.

A few times back and forth and they were moving more smoothly.

"Now we go to the end, and you dip me and kiss me," Priska announced.

Thomas froze. Günther was going to kiss Priska? Just like that? He had the urge to run and cut in. His mouth suddenly felt dry. He was the one who was supposed to kiss Priska. He felt she was doing the same thing she had done with Manfred—encouraging Günther's attention even if it wasn't the kind she wanted. He wondered if she didn't have feelings for him after all, or if, for some reason, she enjoyed creating a kind of love triangle like the one she had talked about in *Mazurka*.

The music inside the ballroom stopped and the crowd clapped. Thomas felt a wave of relief that this would put an end to their dancing, but Priska and Günther kept going just the same. A new song started. It wasn't a tango but that didn't seem to matter to Günther. He danced Priska to the railing and tipped her back. Priska's hair swung as she leaned her head back. Her eyes were wide—perhaps she hadn't expected Günther to follow through.

Thomas felt words sticking in his throat. But it was too late. Günther leaned in and kissed her, loudly enough that Thomas heard the puckering sound. He didn't want to be caught looking and turned away.

Günther pulled Priska upright, and they walked back to Thomas, swinging hands and laughing.

"Well done" was all Thomas could think to say.

Priska grabbed her skirt and curtsied. "Why, thank you,"

she said, letting out a nervous laugh. She turned to Günther and held out her hand, entreating him to bow. Thomas clapped as Günther swept his arms out and dipped his head in a dramatic bow worthy of a stage actor. Thomas wished it *had* only been a charade.

Günther's father pushed open the door to the deck and startled upon seeing his son. "You should be in bed," he said. But he was smiling and looking beyond them. He pointed into the dark night sky. "Look."

They moved to the railing. There, in the distance, was a faint beam of light.

"What is it?" Günther asked.

"A lighthouse on the Bahamas. We're really almost there."

Priska was unusually quiet. Thomas looked at her instead of at the lighthouse, wondering what she was thinking and feeling. The night was balmy, but she wrapped her arms around herself as if she were cold.

Finally Günther's father said, "Come, Günther, your mother and I are turning in." He put his arm around his son, and as they walked away, he added over his shoulder to Priska and Thomas, "You should be in bed *too*."

Günther looked back at Thomas and Priska before following his father.

After they had gone, Thomas said to Priska, "You're quiet." It wasn't like her not to care about the lighthouse. He would have expected her to be jumping up and down.

Priska turned to face him. The wind had wreaked havoc on her hairdo, and her curls fluttered wildly again. Her eyes were bright, even in the dim light. "I wanted *you* to dance with me, not Günther."

"Then why did you ask both of us?"

"I'm not sure."

"If you wanted to dance with me, then why did you—" Thomas tripped over the words he meant to say. Saying out loud that Günther and Priska had kissed would only make it more real.

"Kiss Günther?" Priska said. "I wanted to make you jealous. But he wasn't actually supposed to kiss me. You were." She dropped her gaze to the deck.

"It worked," Thomas said. "I *was* jealous." He stood there, feeling as if the space between them was much larger than it was. Priska had said she wanted to kiss him. This was his chance. He was so close to her, yet he couldn't bring himself to do, or say, anything.

"Thomas?" Priska said.

"Yes?"

"Now is where you kiss me."

She closed her eyes. Thomas stalled, looking at her. Her face was upturned, as it had been in the theater when Max kissed the beautiful young actress. Thomas breathed in, felt his heart pumping in his chest. He leaned closer and then stopped. Priska opened her eyes.

"No. I'm not going to kiss you. Not like this, when you just kissed Günther."

In the flickering light of the ship's lamps, Thomas saw tears in her eyes.

She said, "Don't you ever do anything rash? Something you regret later on?"

"Yes," Thomas said. "You know I do." Although what he regretted most was what he *hadn't* done.

Priska looked away from him, out at the lighthouse again.

"I'm sorry," Thomas said.

She said softly, "I am too."

Chapter Fourteen

The ship was quiet the next day as people stayed in their cabins packing and readying themselves for their new lives. Thomas had little to pack. It would have taken him even less time to arrange his garments in his suitcase if he hadn't come upon the letter he had received from Walter back in the Cherbourg harbor. He studied the handwriting for far too long, wondering if he and Walter would have more in common than their penmanship.

Later he wandered around the ship, which seemed ghostlike for its emptiness. He didn't see Priska once all day and decided to dine in the tourist-class salon that evening. He wondered if in not kissing her, he had made a mistake he would regret forever, yet he knew it wouldn't have felt right.

The ship's Klaxon sounded at four o'clock the next morning. Thomas climbed down from his bunk, dressed quickly, and returned to the tourist-class dining salon. He sat at one of the rows of long wooden tables. Like many of the people around him, he only picked at his food. He knew that the others had little appetite from the excitement of arrival, whereas he was anxious both about seeing Priska and about whether they would be allowed to disembark.

At first the dining hall was unusually quiet, but soon people were leaning close and whispering. The whispers turned louder.

"Did you hear?" Oskar said to Thomas. "We've anchored outside the harbor. Apparently there's some problem."

"Some people have false passes," a woman sitting across from Thomas replied. "Those people are holding us up and putting those of us who paid good money for our passes in jeopardy." She narrowed her eyes at Thomas, as if she knew him to be one of the offenders.

"No, I heard it's something about the *ship's* documents," Herr Kleist bellowed at the woman. He ripped off a huge bite of sausage with his yellowing teeth. "Something about the crew."

Thomas pushed his plate away. *Rumors have some truth to them.* What little appetite he'd had was gone. He remembered how his mother had pressed him to eat the morning he boarded the *St. Francis.* He hadn't been able to eat then either. If they weren't allowed in, she would be devastated. All she wanted was to see him safe. And Priska—Thomas couldn't even imagine how upset she would be. It would turn her whole happy world upside down.

He left the gossip of the dining room to go on deck. It was still mostly dark out. He had hoped to find the ship inching along but it *was* anchored, and he could make out the lights of Havana in the distance.

Thomas walked across the deck, navigating around the deck boys with their mops and buckets. He went to the entrance to the first-class dining hall and looked in. There were the Affeldts. His heart stuttered as he saw Priska. Thomas had expected her to be wearing her frilly white dress. But she was wearing a navy dress he'd never seen before. It hung a little slack on her frame, and Thomas wondered if it was her mother's. Still, she looked grownup in it. It suited her far better than the child's dress. She was so pretty the way she brought her fork delicately to her mouth. To the lips he'd almost kissed. What if he had missed his chance? Looking at her, he had an overwhelming feeling of wanting to protect her, to make sure everything turned out all right.

Professor Affeldt spotted him and waved him over.

Thomas was aware of every step he took, and equally aware that Priska was not looking at him.

"Have you eaten?" Professor Affeldt asked him.

"Yes," Thomas said. "I was up early with the Klaxon."

"Have you heard we're not allowed any further into the harbor?" Marianne said.

"It's just a health check," Priska said, finally looking at him but somehow still not acknowledging his presence. She spoke matter-of-factly, as if she were answering a question in school. "We saw the Cuban doctor come on board. He needs to make sure we're all healthy before we can be admitted."

"Sit with us while we finish up," Professor Affeldt said. "Then we're going to get in line so we can be one of the first on Cuban soil."

"All right," Thomas said, and sat down. He glanced over at Priska but she had turned away from him again.

⸻

Usually Thomas would have been annoyed at having a doctor shine a light in his eyes, jab a wooden stick nearly down his throat, and question him about diseases he might have had. But the doctor was Cuban, not German, and Thomas just wanted to finish the checkup. They were supposed to have their passes stamped immediately after, but they were told to wait. A launch pulled up and Priska and Marianne ran to look at it. Thomas followed and reached them as the launch nestled alongside the ship.

"We heard a launch could be taking us to shore instead of the ship's going all the way into the harbor," Priska informed him, again with an air of indifference.

Three uniformed men climbed out and made their way

onto the ship. A steward met them and shepherded them in the direction of the first-class dining hall, which had emptied of the breakfast crowd.

Marianne said, "It doesn't look like it's going to take us in."

"Be quiet," Priska snapped at her. "What do you know? You're just a child."

Priska turned with a huff. As they followed her back to Professor and Frau Affeldt, Thomas wished he could explain to Marianne why Priska was being so mean. But he actually wasn't sure if it was because of him or because of what was happening.

"Cuban officials just arrived," Priska informed her parents.

Frau Affeldt draped her hand over her eyes. "What more could possibly need to be done before we get off this rotten ship?"

While most everyone else aboard seemed to have gained weight and improved in overall health and complexion, Thomas thought she looked thinner than when they had left Hamburg.

Professor Affeldt waved a hand. He didn't look at any of them as he said, "Just logistics. Paperwork."

Thomas glanced out toward Havana. Now that the sun had come up, he could see the palm trees with their fronds like giant umbrellas, and houses in such unlikely colors as pink and light blue. They were like nothing he'd ever seen before. He tried to imagine walking the Cuban streets, taking in all the new sights, smells, and sounds. He tried to imagine where Walter lived and what kind of food he ate. But it looked so different from any home he knew that it was nearly impossible to do.

"If we need to wait a little longer, we'll wait," Professor Affeldt said. "We are good at waiting." He sighed deeply. "Perhaps too good."

———

By midmorning, the Cuban officials who had come on board started processing papers.

Thomas and the Affeldts hurried to be at the front of the line that soon snaked all around the deck. Around them everyone waited in silence. Lisbeth shushed Margot, as if talking might somehow jeopardize their chances of getting off the ship. The only sounds were Spanish words, the rustling of papers as the officials looked over documents, and the thwump of the stamp. As they came closer to the table, Thomas noticed how Priska's eyes were drawn to the stamp itself. She held her pass firmly between her thumb and palm. When it was her turn, he saw that her hand was shaking as she held out the pass. Once it was stamped, she hurried away. Thomas reached the table and held out his passport and landing card. He looked at the big red "J" on his passport. If they did get off, perhaps soon he could get a new one, without the "J." The official raised his stamp and pressed it down on the landing card. Thomas felt a prickling sensation travel up his spine.

Next he went with the Affeldts to the top of the gangway. Another launch motored toward them. Priska held hands with her father and Marianne.

Marianne pointed to the launch and stood on her tiptoes to see it better. Everyone around them inched forward, waiting for instructions. But no instructions came. Instead another Cuban official boarded the ship and pushed his way through the crowd. "Move aside," he barked.

"What's happening?" Priska asked, her face scrunched up.

"Excuse me, sir," Professor Affeldt called out after the official, who kept going.

"Why aren't we getting off?" Priska said.

Thomas tried to console her by saying, "It must be more paperwork," but she turned from him as if she hadn't even heard him.

No one wanted to give up their place in line, even though it became clear they weren't disembarking soon. A few minutes later the official came back, followed by the three other officials who had come aboard earlier, the ones who had stamped the passes. All four promptly climbed back into the launch and set off for shore. Only one official remained, a heavyset man who stood at the top of the ladder with his arms crossed.

"Wait!" Priska cried. "Where are they going? Come back!"

Herr Kleist elbowed his way to the front of the crowd. He was waving his passport and yelling, "Don't leave, don't leave!"

"What is the meaning of this?" Professor Affeldt asked the remaining official.

He answered in Spanish. Thomas couldn't understand a word of what he was saying, and the sickening feeling inside him was growing. People continued to push to the front and bombard the official with questions, but the answers became shorter. Finally it was just one word: "*Mañana.*"

"What do we do now, Vati?" Priska said.

"We wait," he said again. This time his voice sounded tired.

"Here?"

"For a while, anyway. We don't want to lose our place in line."

By midday the sun was beating down on the deck. Herr Kleist took off his jacket and loosened his tie. Lisbeth, her belly stretching the fabric of her dress, shielded Margot from the glare of the sun. Frau Rosen fanned herself with her hand. Another ship, half the size of the *St. Francis,* pulled up and anchored nearby. Thomas read the name on it: *Arrieta*. Passengers lined its decks, craning their heads to get a glimpse of the city.

"What's that?" Herr Kleist said, pointing.

"Looks like another liner," Frau Rosen replied.

Herr Kleist pulled at his collar. "Another liner? From where? They better not get off before we do."

Thomas saw Priska's shoulders sink. Her cheeks looked sunburnt.

"Are you all right?" he asked her.

"I'm just hot."

"You need to get out of the sun."

"I'm not leaving this very spot."

Thomas took off his hat and offered it to her. "At least put on my hat."

Priska let him set it on her head. She closed her eyes.

He sat down next to her. "You can't be mad at me."

"Why not?"

"First of all, you're the one"—he lowered his voice—"who kissed him. Second of all, you said if you could, you'd go through life without any arguments."

"Well, I guess I was wrong," she said.

Thomas opened his mouth to ask which part she had been wrong about—kissing Günther or going through life without arguments—when Herr Kleist yelled, "They're getting off!"

Thomas jumped up. Priska stood too, teetering on her

feet at first. The passengers on the *Arrieta* were indeed filing off onto a launch. Frau Rosen screamed. Lisbeth started crying, huge sobs that shook her whole body, even her enormous belly.

Professor Affeldt climbed up one of the masts so he was above the panicked crowd. "Listen," he yelled out over everyone. He waved his arms, trying to get their attention. "Listen up! Screaming like this will not advance our cause! Do you want to get off this ship?"

Lisbeth wiped her face on her sleeve. Margot clutched her doll to her chest.

Jürgen said, "Quiet! Listen to the man!"

Herr Kleist fell silent and the rest of the crowd settled too. Professor Affeldt continued, "This could be a good sign. Others are being admitted. Hopefully we will be next. Above all else, we need to stay calm. Remember, there are many people who think we Jews are animals. We need to behave in accordance with all measure of the law. We need to show them the refined and civilized people we are."

Frau Rosen spoke up. "He's right. We must stay calm."

"By asking our questions politely, we will find out the situation at hand," Professor Affeldt added.

The captain had come on deck and was listening to Professor Affeldt. Thomas wondered if he would be threatened or upset by Professor Affeldt's taking charge of his ship, and if he might order him to stop immediately. But

Professor Affeldt finished of his own accord and stepped down, at which point the captain asked to have a word with him on the bridge.

Professor Affeldt walked off with the captain. Behind him, Herr Kleist ranted, "Where do they think they're going?"

"Enough from you!" Frau Rosen snapped.

Herr Kleist scowled but he kept quiet while they waited. Thomas watched Priska, wondering how long she could stay mad at him and whether he would ever get the chance again to kiss her. Her arms were crossed over her chest and her lips were a flat line, as if to say she would stay angry for a long while.

When Professor Affeldt returned, everyone rushed to gather around him.

"What did he say?" Oskar asked.

Herr Kleist wiped at his watery eye. "Yes, you must tell us."

Professor Affeldt motioned for them to calm down. "The captain is forming a passenger committee to serve as a liaison between himself and the passengers, relaying information so as to cut down on the questions and confusion. He has asked me to be on the committee."

"Who else is on it?" Elias asked.

"Herr Seliger, Herr Feuerbach, and Doktor Carell." Oskar rolled his eyes. "All old men."

Professor Affeldt nodded slowly, as if giving himself

time to choose his next words carefully. "The captain made his choice based on what he has observed on the voyage."

"What did he say?" Elias asked. "What's the holdup?"

"Yes, tell us the situation . . . honestly," Frau Rosen added.

"The president of Cuba has issued a decree saying that we cannot land because we do not have visas."

"But we have landing permits," Frau Rosen pointed out.

"Yes, and they are apparently not the same thing."

Elias furrowed his brow. "Then why did they sell them to us and say we would be allowed in?"

"It's a German plot," Oskar said. "I knew it when they made us pay for a return trip, claiming it was just insurance against unforeseen circumstances."

Others added their voices:

"Why can't they at least let us leave?"

"It's not enough to strip us of everything we have?"

"This is just like the Nazis . . . it never stops with them."

Professor Affeldt shook his head. "No, in fact, this seems to have more to do with Cuba. Apparently they don't always do things in a lawful manner."

"What will we do now?" Oskar pressed Professor Affeldt.

"Tomorrow a representative from the American Jewish Joint Distribution Committee in New York City is coming. They are pleading our case."

Oskar insisted, "We need to take action and get this situation resolved."

Professor Affeldt held up a hand to him. "I have said

this many times today and I will say it again . . . all we can do for now is wait."

Professor Affeldt tried to move away but the crowd wouldn't let him, barraging him with more questions. *Would they at least be allowed ashore to visit with their loved ones while everything was cleared up? Did they have enough food and water to last them?*

Thomas shifted around the group, heading for where Priska had been standing on the other side. But once he maneuvered by all the people, she was gone.

Chapter Fifteen

Over the next day, all manner of small boats—rowboats, skiffs, catamarans—anchored alongside the ship. A Cuban man called up to the passengers, offering brightly colored fruit.

"Do you have any pineapples?" Thomas asked.

He held up a coconut and Thomas shook his head. "Pineapple?"

The man offered a bunch of bananas. On the third try, he produced a pineapple. Thomas took a few coins from his pocket. He dropped one down to the man and waited. "More?"

The man nodded.

Thomas dropped another coin down. The man threw the pineapple up to him. Thomas caught it. The sharp points prickled his hands.

Down below, a man in another skiff called up in German, asking for Lisbeth Cohn. Moments later Lisbeth ran to the railing. At first Thomas thought she might go straight over the side of the ship, but she stopped and held out her hands. The man blew kisses to her and told her not to worry. She picked up Margot and, heaving her over her giant belly, held her above the railing. Margot had a puzzled look on her face, and Lisbeth kept repeating through her tears, "There's Vati. Wave to Vati."

Thomas heard Priska's voice behind him. "What craziness."

Thomas held the pineapple toward her. "You said the first thing you would do in Havana was have a pineapple."

She smiled. "Is that a peace offering?"

Thomas raised his eyebrows. "Will it work?"

"Come on," she said. "Let's go find a way to cut this up."

At the bar they asked the bartender for a plate and knife.

"I'll do one better for you," he said, and took the pineapple. He returned moments later with it neatly cored and sliced, accompanied by two bowls of sweet cream. "It tastes delicious with cream on top."

"Thank you," Priska said.

"Yes," Thomas mumbled, still skeptical about trusting any kindness from the crew. "Thank you."

The bartender nodded. "It's the least I can do."

Priska took a bite and proclaimed, "Delicious."

Next to them, a man downed a drink and ordered another brandy and water.

"You're not mad at me anymore?" Thomas asked.

Priska let out an exaggerated sigh. "I guess not."

She smiled and took another bite of pineapple. He thought she seemed oddly happy given what was going on, and he asked, "Aren't you worried about what will happen to us?"

She shook her head. "It'll get sorted out with time. If the landing permits were no good, they wouldn't have given them to us. We wouldn't have kept going if we were just going to have to turn around."

Thomas stared at her. Before they had arrived in the Havana harbor, her outlook had seemed stubbornly optimistic. Now it seemed only foolhardy. He wondered if her father had lied to her about what was happening. Thomas wanted to protect her too, but he wouldn't go so far as to lie to her.

"You don't believe it will all work out?" she said.

"I'm not sure."

Priska swirled the cream in her bowl. "You have to have faith."

"I'm trying to remain hopeful."

"I didn't say hope. I said faith. There's a difference."

Thomas squinted.

Priska explained, "Hope is wishing for something. Faith is believing in something."

She took a few more bites of pineapple, then put her spoon beside her bowl and declared, "I, for one, think we need to do something."

"What do you mean?" Thomas asked. He couldn't imagine how they could do much of anything.

"Something to distract people. I was thinking of a chess tournament. . . . We'll get lots of people to play."

"I'm not sure that's what we need," Thomas said.

"That's precisely what we need," she argued. "Something else to focus on."

Thomas scooped up the remaining bit of cream in his bowl. He had learned there was not much sense in trying to dissuade her when she had an idea in her head. And chess was easier for him than hope or faith. "Well, I suppose we could. . . ."

"Good, now how do we set up a tournament?"

"We'll have four rounds. No one will be eliminated so everyone can keep playing, regardless of how good they are, but as the rounds progress we'll end up with the best players playing each other."

Priska took a last bite and put down her spoon. "Come on, then, we have work to do."

—◦◦◦—

Priska and Thomas split up and canvassed the ship, asking people if they wanted to play in the tournament. Thomas was surprised at how many people said yes. He began to think Priska was right—this was just what they needed. They met up again in the social hall and Priska handed Thomas her list. He scanned the names—Wilhelm and Jürgen, of course; Paul; other men he didn't know; and even a few women. His breath caught in his throat as he read one of the names at the end of her list: *Manfred*. Before Thomas could say anything, Priska said, "I couldn't very well tell him he couldn't play."

"Why not? You could have said it was for passengers only."

"He's probably not very good anyway."

What Priska didn't know, of course, was that Manfred was very good. And for that matter, Thomas didn't see who could beat him. Surely not Jürgen, unless he got lucky. Perhaps Wilhelm. Otherwise it would have to be someone Thomas didn't know, or Thomas himself. Although the idea of playing Manfred again was daunting, it also sent a little spark up Thomas's spine. He might get his chance at revenge after all.

Thomas sighed. "I guess we have no choice but to let him play." He sat down with the list and started drawing up the matchups. In the first round Thomas would play Steffi Safier, a woman he didn't know by name. Manfred would play Paul.

When the matchups were set, they posted the schedule on the bulletin board outside the dining hall and asked the purser to make an announcement over the loudspeaker. A few moments later they heard: "A chess tournament will begin at two o'clock this afternoon in the social hall. The first-round matchups are posted."

Priska gave Thomas a satisfied smile. Even Thomas

couldn't help but be pleased. Instead of standing around, they had set something in motion.

—∞—

In the social hall, they moved tables together and set up the four chessboards. Marianne and Hannelore decorated a banner that read ST. FRANCIS INAUGURAL CHESS TOURNAMENT.

When they had finished, Thomas asked Priska, "Where should we hang it?"

Priska chuckled. "How about right over Hitler?"

They settled for the wall above the tables where the tournament would be played. Priska filled a pitcher and glasses with water and set them on a side table. She surveyed the room and proclaimed, "We're ready."

Thomas checked the clock. They still had half an hour until two. As they waited, Priska asked, "Are you nervous for your first game?"

Thomas shook his head. Perhaps Steffi Safier would be an excellent player, but the only person he was truly nervous about facing was Manfred.

Priska checked the clock again. Still fifteen minutes to go. She rose and made sure the water glasses were filled. With seven minutes to go, there was still no one there, and Priska walked to the chessboards. "Are the pieces all set up right?"

"Yes," he assured her.

"What if no one comes?"

"They signed up. They're coming."

"They could change their minds."

"Then you and I will play each other," Thomas kidded.

"Some game that will be."

The door swung open and in came Paul and Claudia. Priska said a little too loudly, "Welcome to the *St. Francis* Inaugural Chess Tournament!"

"How clever of you to organize this," Claudia said.

Others soon followed, and Thomas saw Priska take a deep breath. Manfred came and stood alone at one side of the room. At five minutes after two, Priska moved into the center of the room. "Thank you all for coming to the *St. Francis* Inaugural Chess Tournament. The first games are set to begin. Good luck to all."

Thomas took his seat across from Steffi Safier. Manfred sat next to him, playing Paul. Steffi Safier reached out to shake Thomas's hand, and they began to play. It was a straightforward and one-sided game, with Thomas defeating her promptly, in only eighteen moves. He was done so quickly that he was able to watch Manfred play Paul. Paul was a nervous player. His eyes darted around the board, and he cleared his throat repeatedly between moves. In comparison, Manfred looked even more poised and calm. Thomas soon saw that Manfred's style hadn't been an aberration. If Thomas held out any hope that Manfred's win against him had been luck, it soon disappeared. Manfred chiseled away at Paul's pawns until they were weak, doubled, isolated, and then ultimately gone. It happened so smoothly, so subtly, that after they had finished, Paul kept staring at the board and rubbing his chin. Finally he shook Manfred's hand and turned to face Claudia.

She pecked him on the cheek. "A tough loss."

Paul blinked. "I don't even know where I went wrong. It just fell apart." He glanced over to where Manfred was pouring himself a glass of water. "He's very good."

Thomas heard Jürgen murmur to Wilhelm, "He'll be the one to beat."

Thomas was still thinking about Manfred as he sat down for his second game. His opponent was a man named Franz, who had won his last game with a brilliant knight sacrifice that had raised a small commotion among the growing number of spectators.

Franz was old enough to be Thomas's grandfather. He had deep-set eyes that made him look intelligent and serious. As they arranged the pieces, Thomas noted how Franz did everything slowly and methodically. Before the game began, he linked his hands together and cracked his knuckles, something Thomas assumed he did before every game. Thomas wondered when that little habit of Franz's had begun. Likely many years ago. Franz had probably played thousands of games and learned from every one of them. Against such an experienced opponent as Franz, Thomas knew he couldn't rely on his own endgame skills—Franz would no doubt be familiar with king and pawn endgames from the thousands of games he'd played. Instead Thomas decided to avoid piece trades, making the game complicated and tactical. In such positions, he could rely on his quick wit and outcalculate the older Franz. With this plan in mind, Thomas opened with the risky King's Gambit, known for its highly tactical nature. As he played the Gambit, Thomas felt confident. He was playing as he imagined Lasker would—using psychology to outwit his opponent before the first move was even played. Franz shrugged as he took Thomas's pawn sacrifice, not rattled by Thomas's aggressive opening choice.

In return for his sacrificed pawn, Thomas had a strong attack, and he worked hard to coordinate his pieces on the kingside. Just as he expected, the game soon became complicated.

"Why did he do that?" Claudia asked behind Thomas.

"Shhh," Franz said, and the crowd tittered before quieting again.

Thomas looked over at Manfred, who was playing Wilhelm. If any player would have the presence of mind to beat Manfred, Thomas believed it would be Wilhelm. But he could see from the board that Manfred was dominating the game. He forced Wilhelm's pawns onto the same-color squares, leaving him practically immobilized and without options. Manfred's space advantage grew larger and larger as Wilhelm trapped himself with his own pieces. It was as if Manfred searched out whatever small weaknesses his opponent showed and capitalized on them. If Wilhelm had proven to be no match for Manfred, then Thomas feared no one could beat Manfred, least of all himself.

Franz cleared his throat. Thomas looked back to the board. It was his move. He rubbed his eyes, trying not to get lost in the web of variations. But he could barely keep track of it all. He would calculate a move four moves deep, only to find the variation irrelevant because of an unexpected move by Franz. Soon pieces began to trade, and Thomas's attack looked to be fading. He glanced over at Manfred again. He wasn't even playing him and Manfred was still affecting his game.

Under the table, Franz tapped his foot. Thomas stretched his neck from side to side. He looked back at the board and there it was. The best move was staring right at him. It was as if the pieces had moved since he had looked away. He played it immediately and looked up at Franz to gauge his reaction.

But Franz's face remained stoic, revealing neither pride nor disappointment as the game continued. Franz went down a bishop, but he didn't seem upset or anxious. Thomas found himself thinking ahead instead of concentrating on the board. He saw Manfred stand up and shake Wilhelm's hand. The game was already over. Manfred had won. Thomas turned back to the board. He took a deep breath but his chest was tight all of a sudden. Everything had fallen apart. Franz had forced a trade of pawns, and now, even winning by a bishop, Thomas wouldn't be able to queen his rook's pawn. He thought hard about ways he could salvage the game, but no progress could be made. As Thomas trapped Franz's king to the eighth rank, Franz looked up at Thomas with the first hint of emotion he had shown during the game. "Stalemate," he said with a wise smile.

"What's that?" Claudia said from behind Thomas. "Did one of them win?"

Thomas shook hands with Franz and stood up to leave, feeling unsteady on his feet. He heard someone telling Claudia that it was essentially a tie. He had not lost. Thomas knew that. But it was little consolation for a game he had thought he would win. Manfred had infiltrated his mind and made him play poorly again.

"That was a bold strategy," Franz said to Thomas. "Starting with the King's Gambit. Impressive."

At Franz's compliment, Thomas felt his anger fade slightly. "Thank you. You were a tough opponent." As he spoke the words, Thomas wondered if he was being too hard on himself. Franz was clearly a very skilled player and more than four times Thomas's age. Perhaps it wasn't such a comedown to have ended in stalemate. Still, if Manfred hadn't wormed his way into Thomas's head, he was sure he would have won.

"I've played a few games in my lifetime," Franz conceded. A smile flickered across his face. "Do you know I saw Lasker beat Tarrasch? Back in '16."

"In Berlin? When Lasker won five straight games after a draw in the first?"

Franz nodded. "Someone has taught you your history. You would have been only a baby in '16."

"I wasn't even born yet," Thomas said. "But my father told me all about Lasker. He used to watch him play at the Café Kaiserhof."

"One of the finest players." Franz tapped the side of his head. "He could read an opponent like no one else."

"My father encouraged me to model my game after Lasker's. He said Lasker didn't always look for the best move but for the practical move."

"Mmm," Franz agreed. "Just so. Maybe you'll be able to see him play someday. If we all make it to America, that is. If we get these Cubans to come through on their promises. Lasker was one of the smart ones—he got out back in '33."

Thomas had heard his father's version of the Lasker-Tarrasch game many times, and each time it was as exciting as if he didn't already know the outcome. Now he wanted to hear Franz's. He leaned forward, forgetting all about the stalemate. "Lasker-Tarrasch, what was it like?"

"First you must consider the circumstances. It was the middle of the World War. Tarrasch had lost one of his sons in the war, and two of his other sons had died as well. He was in an unstable frame of mind. He had the advantage for much of the last game, and it looked as if Lasker was lost. His position was inferior, and he made a blunder on move fourteen that gave Tarrasch an overwhelming edge. Everyone watching that day thought it was all over. But Lasker wasn't the sort to give up. He knew how to play psychological chess, and he made the game complicated to rattle Tarrasch's nerves. It worked. It took him thirty moves of patient fight, but it worked. He won back the advantage and the game."

Thomas glanced out the window. He would have liked to stay and keep talking to Franz, but he noticed the *Ortsgruppenleiter* conferring with Kurt. "Excuse me," Thomas said to Franz. "And thank you again for the game."

Out on deck, Thomas tried to walk breezily past. He heard Holz tell Kurt, "I'll be back in a few hours. Keep a watch on things for me." Thomas glanced at the gangway and saw a launch waiting. Holz leaned close to Kurt and said something that Thomas couldn't hear.

Kurt nodded and saluted. *"Heil Hitler."*

The *Ortsgruppenleiter* answered with his own salute and headed off to the gangway. But before he could set foot on it, Manfred was in front of him, speaking loudly. "No shore leave. For anyone. Captain's orders."

"I'm not just anyone," Holz said.

Manfred repeated, "No shore leave."

"Get the captain," the *Ortsgruppenleiter* ordered.

Manfred turned on his heel, and Thomas wasn't sure whether that was the end of things. He wondered where he could stand without looking as if he was waiting to find out. Someone had left a copy of the shipboard paper on a deck chair. He picked it up and pretended to peruse it. Next to an article praising the pact between Germany and Italy was a notice of a U.S. Navy ship that had sunk during a test dive, killing twenty-three sailors. The paper made the United States seem weak for bungling a practice exercise and managing to kill its own men. Moments later Manfred returned with the captain.

"Do we have a problem?" the captain asked, standing close to Holz.

"You'll have a problem if you do not allow me to go ashore."

Thomas had abandoned the paper to watch intently. The *Ortsgruppenleiter* and the captain were so caught up in each other that Thomas felt certain they wouldn't notice him. There were mere inches between Holz and the captain. Though the captain was shorter, he didn't seem to be any less powerful or to feel particularly intimidated. "No shore leave for anyone until we get this situation settled. This is my ship. My rules."

Holz smirked. "This is the Führer's ship and the Führer's rules. Something you seem quick to forget."

The captain spoke slowly, enunciating each word. "Then you will need permission from the Führer directly."

The *Ortsgruppenleiter* didn't answer. Instead he stormed off. The captain and Manfred turned back toward the bridge, conversing among themselves. Thomas strained to hear but couldn't make out what they were saying.

Priska came on deck. "There you are. What are you doing?"

"The captain won't let Holz go ashore," Thomas said. "And Holz is desperate to go. Why would he care so much unless he's counting on selling whatever he's smuggling?"

"Vati has news . . . ," Priska said. "About our situation."

Thomas knew this should matter more to him, but he was still caught up in what had just happened with the *Ortsgruppenleiter*.

"The Cuban government wants more money to take us. Five hundred American dollars per person."

"That sounds like corruption," Thomas said.

"Maybe, but it means we'll be let in."

"Nobody on this ship has that kind of money. Most of us could barely afford what we've already paid."

"The Joint is working on raising the money. Some businessmen and fellow Jews in America have offered to contribute."

Thomas shook his head.

"You have to have faith, remember?" Priska said.

He smiled at her, for her, but he knew faith was something you had to feel innately—it wasn't something you could will yourself to create.

Chapter Sixteen

As Thomas walked to the social hall the next morning for the second day of the tournament, he noticed how the ship had changed. People on the deck stood in clusters at the railing, talking furtively while pressing handkerchiefs to their eyes. The cushioned deck chairs, which only days before had held sunbathers, now stood empty. The sports deck was similarly barren, the shuffleboard cues and tennis rackets abandoned in a corner. No one swam in the pool, and even the children in the nursery played quietly.

Thomas threw open the door to the social hall to find a large crowd gathered. Here the talk focused on chess: who was to play whom, who would likely win. Priska had been right—the tournament was just what they needed. Thomas too was glad to see the chessboards ready and waiting.

He played Wilhelm while next to him Manfred faced off against Franz. As they determined who would play white, Thomas vowed he would not let Manfred into his head this time. He would play his own game and leave Manfred to play his.

Wilhelm won white and he opened with the Ruy Lopez. He played each move calmly, as if he were completely sure of himself. Thomas admired his style. His father had always told him chess was a confidence game—you had to believe at all times that you could win. If you were ever unsure of yourself, it could kill you. Thomas tried to match Wilhelm's confident style, and after twenty moves their positions were fairly equal.

Thomas surveyed the board. He saw an advantage on the queenside and, pushing up a pawn, began to gain space and initiative. As he envisioned it, Wilhelm would respond with a defensive rook move to the knight file, and Thomas would be well on his way to the win. Thomas felt a strong desire to look over at Manfred and Franz's game, but he forced himself to keep his eyes on his own board.

Across from him, Wilhelm straightened his spectacles. Until then Wilhelm had remained nearly still, so even that minor movement jolted Thomas. Wilhelm calmly moved his king's pawn up two squares. Jürgen groaned from where he was watching behind Thomas.

Thomas swallowed hard. He had been certain Wilhelm would move his rook, and now the move Thomas had planned next had simply evaporated. The whole game as he had seen it developing had changed dramatically with that one move. Thomas heard his father's voice in his head: *An attack on the wing is best met with a counterattack in the center.* Of course. How could he have missed Wilhelm's counterattack? Now, in just one move, the pendulum had swung to Wilhelm's favor.

Thomas returned his attention to the board. He was freezing, which seemed ridiculous since the room was hot and airless. Still, he tried not to shiver. Across from him Wilhelm was maddeningly calm. Thomas told himself that the game was far from over. If he lost, this time he could not blame it on Manfred. For the next eight moves, he focused hard and regained some of his lost ground in the center. He quickly made the game complicated—he would make this hard for Wilhelm. Finally he saw his chance. He found a rook move, and as the position began to simplify again, he was pleased that he'd regained equality.

Wilhelm looked visibly upset for the first time since the game had begun. He took his spectacles off and polished them, then mumbled under his breath. The position was equal, but Wilhelm continued to play the game as if he were winning. He moved his queen deep into enemy territory, trying to intimidate Thomas.

But Thomas played on Wilhelm's frustrations, allowing Wilhelm to advance farther and farther into his territory. Wilhelm moved his queen all the way down to the end of the board, ignoring his own king's defenses.

Thomas tried not to smile as he felt the game turning

back in his favor. His queenside pawns were now very strong, and he started pushing them up the board. It took only moments for Wilhelm to realize what was happening, and he quickly tried to bring back his pieces in time to stop Thomas's pawns. But it was too late. Thomas moved a pawn up to the seventh rank. Behind him Jürgen whispered, *"Ja, gut."* Wilhelm countered by taking Thomas's knight, but Thomas was not troubled because he knew that the pawn would eventually turn into a queen, which was worth far more. And two moves later it did just that. He had won.

"Good game," Wilhelm said, extending his hand. "You played smart. You're learning."

He heard Priska call, "Thomas!" He turned to see her rushing toward him. He didn't have a moment to celebrate or even to check on Franz and Manfred, who were still playing. He thought she was there to congratulate him but instead she said, "It's your brother. He's come alongside in a boat. He's been asking for you."

Thomas jumped up, for the moment forgetting all about his win.

"Come on," Priska said. "I'll show you."

Thomas hurried after her, not even feeling his feet as he ran. When he reached the railing, he looked down at the water, searching the many boats bobbing alongside the *St. Francis*.

Walter called out, "Thomas Werkmann!"

Thomas saw him and his heart surged. He had been too young when Walter had left to really remember him; nevertheless Walter looked familiar. Thomas thought maybe it was because Walter's dark, thick hair looked like his father's. His father—he would have been proud of how he'd just played. He had kept his wits about him and not once made a rash move.

"Walter!" Thomas called back so loudly that it scratched his throat.

"Thomas!"

Now Thomas understood why the people he had seen calling down to family in the boats looked as if they might jump straight over the railing. It was all he could do to keep himself on board.

"You'll be let in . . . have patience. We're doing everything we can," Walter said.

Thomas nodded, feeling heat behind his eyes. Seeing Walter made it real that he had someone waiting for him. He had family. It also made him miss his father terribly. He wondered what Walter would have done if he had been the one to come upon their father being beaten in the street. But there was nothing anyone could have done, Thomas told himself, as he had many times before.

Thomas wasn't sure what more he could say to Walter. It was too far away to hold a real conversation. Still, he was content just to look at him, to know he was there. But after a while the man with the skiff exchanged a few words with Walter.

"There are many others waiting to come out," Walter called to Thomas. "I have to go back."

Thomas held out his hand, offering a gesture between a wave and an attempt to somehow reach his brother.

"We'll be together soon," Walter added.

The man started the motor. Walter waved and Thomas waved back, his whole body swaying. He watched his brother disappear, and wondered if he would ever see him again.

Thomas turned from the railing to see two stewards watching him.

"Is something wrong?" he asked.

"Just a precaution," one said.

Before Thomas could ask what they meant, they had headed off down the deck. He turned to Priska, who was still next to him.

"Your brother seems wonderful," she said.

"Do you know what that was all about? The stewards?"

"I heard Vati say some people are threatening to jump overboard and swim to shore."

Thomas looked back out to where Walter had just been. Swimming to shore didn't sound like such a bad idea. If it would only work. But they would no doubt be brought right back to the ship.

After lunch Professor Affeldt enlisted Thomas and Priska's help. "The Joint wants us to compile a list of relatives of passengers who live in the United States. Then they can use the list to try to persuade the United States to let us in."

"Have they given up on Cuba?" Thomas asked. He thought of his brother waving to him. He had no family in America.

"No, this is just in case."

Professor Affeldt handed them paper and pen. "Work together. Get names, relationship to passengers, and addresses, if possible."

The first person Thomas and Priska saw was Frau Rosen. "Let's skip her," Priska suggested.

"No, we have to ask everyone," Thomas said. He took the paper and pen from her. "I'll do it."

Priska grabbed the paper back from him. "If anyone is doing it, it's me. I'm not watching you stutter and make eyes at her."

Thomas stopped and turned to her. "You're much more beautiful than anyone on this ship."

Priska smiled, and together they approached Frau Rosen. Priska said in her most pleasant voice, "Excuse me, *gnädige Frau.*"

"What do you scoundrels want?" She glared at Thomas and he immediately looked at the deck. Then he thought Priska might assume he was looking at Frau Rosen's legs, so he turned his eyes to the harbor.

"As you may know, my father is on the passenger committee," Priska began. "We're compiling a list of relatives of passengers who live in the United States. Would you happen to have a relative there?"

Frau Rosen straightened. "Yes, indeed, my husband."

"Wonderful," Priska said. "May we have his name and address?"

Frau Rosen gave them the information and Priska wrote it down.

"Are we going to make it?" Frau Rosen asked.

Thomas was taken aback, as if they could somehow know the fate of a whole ship. But by this point, everyone was looking to someone—anyone—to reassure them. "We don't really know any more than you do," Thomas said.

Priska smiled. "God willing."

They thanked Frau Rosen, but before they left, Priska said, "Also, I must apologize . . . about the soap on the door handle."

Frau Rosen reached out and pinched Priska's waist. "Such a pretty girl. You will break many boys' hearts." She winked at Priska. "As for the prank, I was young once too, no?"

They spoke to thirty people, a fraction of the nine hundred passengers on board. But it was a start. They slumped down on a bench for a few moments.

A launch came up alongside the ship. Thomas stood to get a closer look. "It can't be."

"What is it?" Priska asked. She stood up too and shielded her eyes from the sun. "Holz."

"He must have received permission from the Führer himself."

The launch came closer and Thomas cursed under his

breath. There was no doubt—it was him. The launch pulled up to the gangway. The *Ortsgruppenleiter* came aboard.

"He looks the happiest I've ever seen him," Priska said.

"Because he's probably just sold everything he stole and made a fortune for the Reich. A fortune to spend on the war effort. If Hitler himself overruled the captain, then Holz has to be smuggling for the Reich."

"He still has the cane." She turned to Thomas.

"That's probably where the money's hidden now."

"What are we going to do?"

"I don't know yet."

Thomas's eyes were glued to that cane. He opened and closed his fists. Somehow he would get his hands on it.

Priska checked her watch. "I should go see my father. And you need to get ready for the final game."

Thomas mumbled, "Yes," still preoccupied with the *Ortsgruppenleiter.*

"You play Manfred next. He's undefeated. He's been playing very well."

Thomas snapped, "Whose side are you on?" But he immediately apologized. "I'm sorry. Seeing Holz—I just can't believe he got permission from Hitler." Thomas ran a hand through his hair. It meant whatever Holz had was extremely valuable. It must have been worth hundreds of thousands of reichsmarks. All Jewish money that would go to funding the Reich and the war.

Priska said gently, "I'll be back to watch you play, after I check in with Vati."

In the remaining hour before the game, Thomas's thoughts shifted from the *Ortsgruppenleiter* to playing Manfred. Since he was undefeated, Manfred was winning the tournament. Thomas, with no losses and only the one stalemate, was in close second. If he beat Manfred, he would have enough points to win the tournament. Winning the tournament didn't matter as much to Thomas as beating Manfred; it just happened that with one came the other.

Thomas imagined that Manfred would play an opening similar to the one he'd used in their first game. He remembered the advice Wilhelm had given him: respect his style but play the game as you have been schooled to play it.

The room was filled with people as Thomas sat down across from Manfred. He determined to simply play chess this time. He didn't want to look at Manfred, let alone talk to him. But there was Manfred, smiling at him. "We get to play again."

"Yes," Thomas replied. He tried to pretend he hadn't been waiting for this moment since the last time they had played. He tried to pretend that this didn't feel crucial to him, but the crowd wasn't helping. Behind him, people whispered and murmured, adding an intensity to the game before it had even begun. There was also something unsettling about knowing that every move he made would be judged by so many people. To make himself feel better, though, Thomas reminded himself that everyone wanted him to win. Everyone wanted nothing more than to see Thomas beat Manfred.

Manfred leaned back in his chair. The crowd hushed as he pushed his queen's pawn up two squares. He didn't lift the pawn, or even look at it; he stared at Thomas as he made the move. And when Thomas challenged his center, Manfred immediately played his bishop's pawn up, entering one of the most daring openings: the Queen's Gambit. Before, Manfred had neglected the center and played like Nimzowitsch, but now he challenged Thomas in one of the most popular and testing lines in chess. Thomas took a deep breath. He knew that those gathered couldn't possibly understand what was really going on between him and Manfred. They didn't know that Manfred had beaten him before while playing unconventional moves and now he was revealing that the whole time he had known the classical systems. They didn't know that he and Manfred had fought over Priska. But they did know that this was a game of passenger against crew, of Jew against Nazi.

Thomas didn't dare look at Manfred after the first moves. Instead he bit his bottom lip and managed to make the next two moves with a steady hand. It was important to show Manfred he was not afraid.

Manfred moved out his bishop and, when Thomas attacked it, retreated it as if he had played the opening for years and years. Thomas sighed. He could do nothing to surprise Manfred. Thomas reached for his queen's bishop's pawn—he always pushed a pawn here. But he stopped short. He could see Manfred frowning at him as his hand hovered over the piece.

"What's he waiting for?" Claudia whispered behind him.

"He's already stuck." Thomas recognized Kurt's voice and looked up to see him standing behind Manfred.

Thomas brought his hand back to cup his chin and let out a sharp exhale. He tried to figure out what Manfred was thinking and how well Manfred actually knew the Queen's Gambit. Thomas could play the queen's bishop's pawn as he usually did. If it worked, the momentum would swing swiftly in his favor. But if Manfred was expecting the move, it would only bring Thomas trouble.

Thomas could feel his knee shaking under the table, and he didn't dare take his hand off his chin until he regained his composure. The spectators were starting to chatter. Thomas was thinking too long for such a normal position. His mind ricocheted between the departure from his mother in Hamburg, his father's bloody face, and Priska's explanation of the difference between hope and faith. Then suddenly, a push of a knight and there was only chess. He could have been playing his father in the back room of the shop at home. The spectators disappeared. His racing mind calmed. The pieces, in their beautiful sculpted simplicity, stared back at him as if they knew no time or place. With his knight move, he had initiated an opening called Lasker's Defense. His father had taught him the move, invented by Lasker himself.

Thomas didn't make the move quietly, as he had done in the past. He picked up the knight and moved it firmly onto the square, as if to tell Manfred and everyone else that Thomas would be the one controlling this game. For the first time since the game started, Thomas looked up and met Manfred's eyes. Manfred nodded, acknowledging the move but not deterred by it.

The game progressed into a test of nerves and a battle of endurance. "Live to fight," he kept telling himself. They played the next few moves quickly—Manfred making threat after threat and Thomas coolly quelling the pressure and playing for small advantages. Manfred's moves began to slow, and he let out deep breaths as the position became difficult for both sides. It looked as though Thomas might lose, but he kept finding moves to save himself for a bit longer. Finally Manfred made a move that Thomas didn't expect, and the crowd oohed. Thomas looked up and saw Professor Affeldt, who nodded at him. He looked back to the board. He needed to defend a pawn, but if he did, Manfred would be able to mount a serious and perhaps unstoppable attack.

Then another idea occurred to Thomas. Instead of defending, he'd let Manfred take the pawn. It was his only hope, so he tossed his queen up the board, starting an attack himself—knowing that if he should fail, he would be going into an endgame a pawn down and nearly facing defeat. Manfred took the pawn, and suddenly the momentum had shifted. Now Manfred was on the defensive, and Thomas's attack kept growing stronger. Losing the pawn had galvanized him to play the game as if it were his last. He could see the lost pawn, off to Manfred's side, and he shifted in his seat to feel his father's pawn in his pocket before making his next move.

As the game went on, Manfred kept his eyes on the board. It was the first time Manfred seemed to have to puzzle out each move, while Thomas started to play the best moves he'd ever made in his life. His knights came in with precise support from his bishops, and his queen tore open files and diagonals. Then suddenly, Thomas leaned back to see a completely won position. All he had to do was sacrifice his queen. He played it with a moment's hesitation, second-guessing his calculation but not for long enough to stop him. Perhaps Manfred had outwitted him again and Thomas was not seeing things as clearly as he thought he was. Manfred took the queen and Thomas made his next move, saying in almost a whisper, "Checkmate."

The crowd burst into cheers. Thomas stood up to shake Manfred's hand but before he could, everyone was upon him. Jürgen clapped Thomas on the back. Priska kissed him on the cheek.

"Well done," Wilhelm said.

After accepting everyone's congratulations, Thomas searched the room for Manfred. No matter what he felt about him, he should shake his hand. His father had always told him that no matter how much he disliked an opponent, it was important to show him proper respect. But Manfred was gone.

Professor Affeldt spoke up. "Friends, I have an important announcement to make and the timing seems rather fitting. The captain has decided we will set off for the United States tonight."

Another, louder cheer went up. Frau Rosen hugged Wilhelm. Even Herr Kleist was smiling. "This is better than we could have ever planned!" he said. "Straight to the United States, no waiting for our numbers to come up. This is what I've been saying we should do all along."

Priska was beaming too. "Isn't this great?" she said to Thomas.

"Yes," he said, although there was Walter to think of, waiting for him in Cuba. And his rational side knew that just because they were headed toward the United States didn't mean they would be granted entrance.

Chapter Seventeen

Priska borrowed her father's camera. As the ship cruised the Florida coastline, they posed for photograph after photograph: Thomas and Günther halfway up one of the masts; Priska, Ingrid, and Marianne grinning in a lifeboat.

"Now everyone together!" Priska called. "Gather around the life ring."

They filled in around the life ring, which read ST. FRANCIS. "Not too close or we won't be able to see the letters on it," Priska instructed.

"You should be in the picture too," Ingrid said. "Wait." She hurried off and returned with Paul, who said he would take the picture.

Priska handed Paul the camera and ran to join the group. She slipped in beside Thomas.

"Smile!" Paul said.

"Say 'America'!" Priska suggested.

They all cried, "America!"

Just before the shutter clicked, Thomas glanced at Priska. He knew he was caught on film that way—the only one not looking at the camera.

Paul handed the camera back to Priska and they all gathered at the railing. Priska pointed into the distance. "Another ship."

When it came closer, the lettering alongside it was visible: U.S. COAST GUARD. Priska waved at an officer standing on the bridge. "They must be coming to guide us in."

The officer didn't wave back.

"Not very friendly, is he?" she said as the ship motored alongside them. "But President Roosevelt is a wonderful man and Vati says he's sure to let us in." She dug into her pocket. "I've been working on a letter to Eleanor Roosevelt too." She held the paper out to Thomas. "What do you think?"

Before Thomas read the letter, he glanced again at the Coast Guard ship. Why hadn't the officer waved back?

Dear Frau Roosevelt,

    Have you ever had to leave your home against your will? Can you imagine leaving your school, your friends, your cat? Worse than that, many of us had to leave family behind: mothers, fathers, grandparents, cousins. But we carried on because

we had faith. Faith that we would soon be in a place
where our parents could smile and laugh again.
Where we would not be scared of a knock at the
door, or of going into town and never coming back.
We hoped to find that place of refuge in Cuba, but
now we turn our eyes to your great country. You
have children of your own and are a compassionate
woman. Please help us. Please give us a place
where we can be safe and happy again.

Yours truly,
The children of the St. Francis

Thomas was aware of her eyes on him the whole time he was reading. He kept looking at the paper after he had finished, not wanting to meet her gaze. The hum of the Coast Guard ship rattled in his ears, giving him a bad feeling.

Finally he said, "It's well done."

"Thank you," she said, smiling.

She waved again at the officer on the bridge. "You can wave back!" she called out, but her voice was lost in the noise of the engines.

Before dinner, Thomas found Professor Affeldt. "The U.S. ship that's running alongside us . . . it's not guiding us in, is it?"

He rubbed his forehead. "No. It's keeping us out."

"They don't want us either? Don't they understand we'll be sent back?"

Professor Affeldt moved his hand from his forehead to his chin. "I'm going to be honest with you, Thomas. I worry that this whole trip was a ruse on the part of Germany—to say they tried to let us go and treated us properly. So they could point to this ship as an example to the world and say, 'See, no one wants those Jews in their countries either. Not Cuba, not even America.'"

"But what about the captain? I thought he was a decent man—why would he have ever gone along with that?" Thomas asked.

"I'm not sure he had any knowledge of what was going on. Either that or he had no choice." Professor Affeldt put a hand on Thomas's shoulder. "Don't tell her yet. We're still pleading our case. I don't want her to know until she absolutely has to."

Thomas nodded. He thought of Priska waving to the officer on the bridge of the Coast Guard ship. Her voice fading into the sound of the engines. The last thing he wanted was to tell her.

That night Thomas and Priska met on deck. The moon was nearly full and it lit up the deck.

"What a moon!" Paul said, leading Claudia out to the

railing not far from Thomas and Priska. A moment later they were no longer looking at the moon.

"All they do is kiss, those two," Thomas said.

"Is that so bad?" Priska asked.

"No," Thomas admitted.

Priska wrapped her arms around herself as if she had just gotten a chill. "Did you hear Lisbeth had her baby? A girl. Emma Cohn. She and the baby are both healthy."

"That's wonderful," Thomas said, but he knew his voice sounded distracted. He couldn't get the conversation with Professor Affeldt out of his head. He wasn't sure how much longer they could keep what was happening from Priska.

Priska continued, "She didn't name her after the ship—so much for tradition."

Thomas was looking at Priska but he could no longer see her face. Only moments before, the deck had been brightly illuminated almost as if it were day; now it was dark. The moonlight was gone. Thomas felt overcome with a sickening feeling.

Priska noticed the darkness too. She looked at the sky. "Where did the moon go?"

"Let's go inside," Thomas said. "You're cold."

"I'm fine," she said. "But the moon—"

Thomas tried to take her hand and lead her inside. But she shook him off and headed down the deck. As he went after her, he hoped the moon had just snuck off behind a cloud. But they emerged onto the port side to find it lit up as the starboard side had been moments before. And there was the moon above them, as if it were mocking them, playing games at their expense. When really Thomas knew that it was not the moon that had moved in the sky but the ship that had reversed course.

"We've turned around," Priska said flatly. "We're going back to Germany."

Thomas braced himself for her tears. He tried to think of what he could say to console her.

She stared out at the sea, not crying, her eyes wide.

"Priska," he said gently.

"Go ahead. Tell me you knew it all along." She turned to him and brushed her hair from her face. "This whole time you thought I was an idiot or a baby who couldn't see the truth. I knew as much as you. In Germany, my parents fought all the time. They were both having affairs. My father, I think, just because he was so sad and lonely, but my mother . . . she was in love with another man. If we go back . . . you see, this was our only hope. A new start, a new home. This was our chance to make it work somehow. If we go back, they'll divorce. I'm sure of it."

Thomas felt as if he were seeing a whole new Priska. A Priska who was not innocent or carefree. Who knew everything but chose to see things the way she wanted to. Yet if she were as worldly as she claimed to be, she would see that going back to Germany meant much worse things than her parents divorcing. Most people on board wouldn't have homes to return to. Many would be taken back to camps. War was surely imminent. Then again, perhaps she knew as much, and her family's happiness meant more to her than even her own life.

"I wanted us to make it too," he said. "You have to believe that."

She pressed the heels of her hands to her forehead. He moved to her and put his arm around her.

"What will we do, Thomas? What will we do if we're sent back? At least you have your mother waiting for you. . . ."

Thomas shook his head. "I'm not going home."

"What do you mean?"

"She's better off without me."

Priska's face was pinched tight. "What will you do? Where will you go?"

Thomas shrugged. "It doesn't matter."

"You'll come with us," she said, perking up.

Thomas smiled faintly at her. "No."

"Why wouldn't you go home? I don't understand."

He swallowed hard. He didn't expect her to understand what he was about to say. How could anyone understand who had not lived through what he had lived through? But still, he felt he needed to try to explain it to someone. "I should have done something. I just let them take him away. I didn't even tell him how much I loved him." If Thomas had had the choice, he would have gladly sold his soul to the devil, as Faust had, in exchange for his father being allowed to escape.

Thomas waited for her to call on all the arguments he had marched through his head many times before: *You would have only made it worse for him. You would have risked your life and your mother's life too. You had no choice. He knew you loved him. He was proud of you for what you did. For how you stayed strong.*

Instead of saying any of those things, which never helped when he told them to himself, she took his hand and squeezed so hard it hurt.

Chapter Eighteen

Professor Affeldt stood under the portrait of Hitler. He waited patiently, looking out over the social hall until the packed room was quiet. He cleared his throat and began, "I am here to confirm that the United States, Canada, and the many other countries we contacted have denied our request for admittance. We are heading back to Europe."

Next to Thomas, Elias called out, "Europe or Germany?" People turned to see who had spoken.

"Right now we don't know," Professor Affeldt replied. "The plan and the hope is that we will not go to Germany. We are traveling slowly so the Joint can continue to negotiate on our behalf."

"Is there a plan, or only a hope?" Oskar said from where he stood next to his brother.

"We are running out of hope," Elias added.

"What did the United States say?" Frau Rosen asked.

Oskar jutted out his chin. "Yes, what reason did they give for not taking us?"

"They said it was a matter for the Cuban government, not the United States," Professor Affeldt replied. "We need to be patient. We on the committee are doing the best we can."

Elias shook his head. "I say we do what we should have done a long time ago—take matters into our own hands."

A few passengers mumbled in agreement. "Hear, hear," someone said.

Elias continued, "If we go back to Germany, many of us will go straight into camps. Perhaps they'll send us all."

"He's right," another passenger called out.

Professor Affeldt raised his hands to quiet the grumbling crowd. "Mutiny is not the answer."

"Then what is?" Oskar demanded. "Tell me, tell *us,* what is?"

"We are composing radiograms to send to influential public figures. If anyone would like to contribute money to send the radiograms, it is greatly needed."

Oskar raised his voice. "I say enough! We have no money left, and no patience. Anyone who feels as my brother and I do, meet out on the deck."

Oskar and Elias stormed out of the room. A few of the younger passengers followed. Professor Affeldt waited until the crowd had quieted again. "Friends," he said, "rashness will get us nowhere."

When Professor Affeldt finished his speech, he tried to move through the crowd to where Thomas stood with Priska. Thomas saw him studying Priska, searching her face to see how she was holding up. People swarmed around him, asking more questions, and he couldn't make it across the room. Priska slipped outside and Thomas followed her.

"Don't try to cheer me up," she said. "That's all my father tries to do."

"Me? Cheer you up?"

Priska smiled faintly.

"I actually need your help," Thomas said.

She looked at him. "With what?"

"Holz. I'm going to get his cane."

She let her gaze drop to the deck. "I'm all done with pranks. Plus, what does it matter anymore, Thomas?"

"This isn't a prank. This is a mission. We can stop him. If we do nothing else, we can stop him from taking that money back to the Reich."

"Money we don't even know actually exists. Just because he stole an old lady's cigarette case . . ."

"I'm sure about this. And I wouldn't ask if I didn't need your help," Thomas said. "I need the key to his stateroom so I can sneak in when he's asleep. I've thought about it over and over, and the only person who can get the key is you."

"How?" She raised her eyebrows, as if she could hardly imagine herself as useful, let alone crucial.

"As captain's steward, Manfred must have a master key. You go to his room late, tell him you've managed to lock yourself out and your father will kill you if he finds you out so late at night. You ask to use his key."

Thomas knew that what he was asking Priska to do was dangerous. What if Manfred tried to have his way with her? It would be late at night, with no one around. But he saw no other way to get the key.

"Will you do it?" Thomas asked.

"Yes," she said.

They decided to wait a few days, hoping things would settle down on the ship. For after the United States turned them away, people went further into despair, some even threatening suicide. Oskar and Elias pushed for mutiny. Rumors trickled down that the captain might try to run the ship aground off the coast of Britain. Due to a food shortage, the meals on board were reduced to a fixed menu. During this time, Thomas concentrated on Holz, keeping track of him and especially studying his nightly routine. He typically turned in at nine, and not once did he reemerge after going into the stateroom he had all to himself on A Deck, an apparent perk of being a delegate of the Nazi Party.

Finally, as they sailed closer and closer to Germany, it

seemed as if people resigned themselves to what lay ahead. Three days before they would be back in Germany, Thomas told Priska it was time.

That night at 11:45, Thomas waited for her at the *Ortsgruppenleiter*'s door. He checked his watch. How long could it possibly take for Priska to get the keys from Manfred? Five minutes, ten minutes at most? They had gone over what she should say—how she would convince him that she needed the key herself, then arrange to leave it at the end of the hall for him. She'd say he shouldn't come with her because her father was a night owl and if he caught her with him, she didn't even want to imagine what would happen.

But it had been twelve minutes and there was no sign of her. Thomas silently cursed himself. He would give her five more minutes and then he would go check on her. In his head he saw Manfred pulling her into his room and closing the door behind him. Three minutes, no more. He couldn't wait five. He stared at the second hand on his watch—it went around twice. He couldn't wait any longer. He headed off down the hall, only to run into her.

"Where are you going?" she asked.

"Are you all right?"

She held up the key. She pressed it into his hand and whispered, "Good luck."

This time, he acknowledged, he would need luck.

As he walked to the door, he thought about the risk he

was about to take. But he was determined to get the cane, and he didn't care what happened if Holz woke and caught him. His father was likely dead. He would not be going back to live with his mother, no matter what Priska had said. He would get off the ship in Hamburg and stay there. He would live on the streets until he was picked up and taken away. The best he could hope for might be ending up at Dachau himself and finding his father. Yes, he had little to live for.

Still, his hand trembled as he slid the key into the lock. It clicked open. The room was much cooler than Thomas's own cabin, a benefit of the ventilation on A Deck, and it was quieter too. Thomas would have to be silent. He waited for his eyes to adjust to the dark. Soon he could make out the bed and the *Ortsgruppenleiter*'s shape under the covers. A man with a true injury would likely have his cane by his bed, but Thomas did not see it there. He breathed a silent sigh when he noticed it against the divan. He walked toward the cane, keeping his eyes on it. He reached the divan and bent down for the cane. His hand was on it when Holz rolled over. Thomas froze. Should he grab it and run, or wait to make sure the man was asleep? Holz rolled once more, rustling the bedding. Thomas didn't dare move now. He waited until his heart had quieted ever so slightly in his chest. He could do this. He knew he could. But he couldn't wait much longer. The longer he waited, the more likely he was to reveal himself by coughing or even just by breathing too loudly. Holding the cane close to his body, he crept out and eased the door shut behind him. It was tempting to take a moment to recover himself, but Thomas knew he couldn't waste time. Holz could wake at any moment and find the cane gone.

Thomas ran to the top deck. He could simply toss the cane overboard, but he yearned to know how to open it and find out what was inside. He checked the very bottom of the cane first—the one place he had not really examined the first time. There was a small groove. It looked as if it could be pried open with a tool. But Thomas had no such tool handy. A ventilation shaft nearby had sharp edges. Thomas positioned the cane against the edge of the shaft and tried to jimmy it open. He was near giving up when, on the fifth try, the bottom of the cane popped off. Just as he had guessed, it was hollow. He wiggled a finger inside. At first he felt only wood, but then his finger caught on something that rustled. Banknotes—he was sure he had been right. But as he slid the papers out, he saw they were nearly transparent.

He held them up to the deck light. Where he had expected to see numbers, he saw architectural drawings of planes. All the words were written in English. Thomas could make out only a few at the bottom: U.S. AIR FORCE. It took him a few moments to realize what these documents were—blueprints of U.S. fighter planes. Holz wasn't a thief, he was a spy. Another Nazi spy in America must have smuggled the papers into Cuba and handed them off to the *Ortsgruppenleiter,* who was taking them back to Hitler.

But they would not get their hands on them. The thin sheaves tore easily. Thomas ripped them into tiny pieces and threw them overboard. He watched as they fluttered off over the sea before disappearing into the dark. Thomas was about to let the last few pieces go when he heard loud footsteps.

He turned to see Holz running toward him, no longer feigning injury.

Thomas braced himself for the impact of his body, or a punch, but Holz grabbed Thomas around the throat and pushed him up against the railing. The wood bit into his back and Thomas heard the top rail groan under the pressure. He felt it give slightly behind him. Holz pushed harder.

Thomas gripped the *Ortsgruppenleiter*'s hands with his own, clawing for air as the man shouted at him. Holz squeezed harder and Thomas was certain he would die. He tried kicking his shins, but he felt like a small dog trying to jump up on someone. The world around him started to go fuzzy.

When Kurt had punched him, Thomas had been almost grateful for the pain. He had wanted more and would have had his fair share of bruises if Priska hadn't pulled him away. All along on the voyage, Thomas had been inviting danger with his smart remarks. Only now he didn't want any more of it. Before, he had wanted to suffer, perhaps as his father had, as he had let his father do. But now he wanted the pain to stop. He would do anything to live through this. A quote from Goethe ran through his head: *It is easier to die than to endure a harrowing life with fortitude.* He did not want to take the easy way out.

But no one else besides Priska knew what he was doing, and he had told her to stay in her room. He had involved her too much already. Thomas stopped struggling, hoping to conserve any strength he had left.

The lack of oxygen made him not trust the next image he saw—that of Manfred rushing upon them, tearing Holz from Thomas and throwing him to the ground. Thomas slumped down against the railing. He gasped for air, coughing and sputtering. His throat ached and his chest burned.

Manfred shouted at the *Ortsgruppenleiter,* "This man is one of our passengers."

"He's a Jew," Holz said. "His life will be over soon enough."

He came at Thomas again. In the split second that Thomas had to process the fact that the attack was resuming, he realized his best chance was surprise. He gathered every last bit of energy inside him, and as the *Ortsgruppenleiter* reached for him, Thomas jumped up, slamming him in the stomach. The blow must have knocked the wind out of him because Thomas now had *him* against the railing. Manfred rushed forward just as Holz was coming back to himself, gasping for air. Manfred landed a hard punch, and all of a sudden there was a loud cracking sound. It took Thomas a moment to understand that it wasn't bones breaking but the railing giving way. The *Ortsgruppenleiter* fell backward, and before Thomas or Manfred could even think of reaching out for him, he disappeared and they heard a splash below.

At first Thomas was certain that people would hear Holz's screams, but it was only moments later that the cries were fainter. Moments after that, they could no longer hear anything but the sea. Even if they had wanted to throw him a life ring, Thomas didn't know how they could have acted fast enough to reach him. Manfred and Thomas were left staring at the water.

The only noise besides the engine was Thomas's labored breathing. He fell to his knees, from pain and exhaustion, and from shock at what had just happened.

"Thomas?" Manfred said. "Are you all right?"

Thomas swallowed, his throat throbbing. He tested his voice. "Yes," he managed. His voice was hoarse but usable.

Thomas tried to return to breathing normally, but it was impossible to take anything more than shallow breaths. Manfred waited with him, and after a while Thomas tried to stand. They both stared at the broken railing.

Manfred said, "I'll tell the captain the truth. That it was an accident."

Manfred sounded calm but he paced the deck. Thomas moved to where the *Ortsgruppenleiter* had fallen over and looked down, but there was nothing to see but water.

"Why should I trust you?" he asked, although he knew he really had no choice. If Manfred wanted to pin Holz's death on him, he easily could. Keeping the *Ortsgruppenleiter* from killing Thomas was one thing, but killing the *Ortsgruppenleiter* was another entirely. Manfred certainly hadn't meant to kill him, and he could be in a lot of trouble from very high up in the Nazi Party if he were blamed for his death.

Manfred walked toward him. Thomas glanced back at the railing, realizing he had unknowingly put himself in a vulnerable position. Manfred was only a few steps away from him. All that separated Thomas from the sea below was the splintered rail. How hard would it be for Manfred to push him overboard?

"You and I are not so different," Manfred said.

Thomas could feel the breeze off the water behind him. "How so?" He imagined Manfred would say that he too loved Priska, but instead he said, his voice scratchy, "No one here knows my mother is a Jew. I am a Jew."

At first Thomas thought this must be some kind of trick. But when he met Manfred's gaze, he knew the man was sincere.

"I ran away from home when I was your age and got a job on this ship. The crew became my second family, a happier family than I had left behind. At first I thought I would someday tell them where I came from, but as things worsened and the hatred for the Jews grew, I knew I couldn't risk telling."

"No one knows?" Thomas asked.

"The captain knows." Manfred smiled, acknowledging that it was most unusual that the captain should know and not care. "He's taken me under his wing. He made me captain's steward to protect me. Now you know my secret too. And now I know why Priska wanted the key. I knew she didn't lock herself out. Some inane story she told me."

"But you gave it to her anyway?" Thomas said.

"She needed it for some reason. That was good enough. I knew she wouldn't do any harm." Manfred paused and then asked, "What was it that you threw overboard?"

Thomas looked at Manfred, gauging whether to tell him. He had just saved his life and admitted that he was a Jew. What more could Thomas want? But he was still keenly aware of the broken rail at his back. "Blueprints of U.S. planes. He must have picked them up in Havana."

Manfred nodded.

"Did the captain know the *Ortsgruppenleiter* was a spy?"

"Yes. But not until he was already on board the ship; otherwise the captain would have quit. I imagine this is his last voyage—mine too." Manfred stepped back and

Thomas was able to move away from the hole in the railing. He realized he was shaking all over.

"Will you be all right?" Manfred asked.

"Yes," Thomas managed. "Thank you." Those two words didn't seem like enough for what Manfred had done for him. But it was hard to be grateful to someone about whom Thomas was still unsure.

Manfred started to walk away, but he stopped and turned back. "I didn't think you would sacrifice that pawn."

"I didn't sacrifice it," Thomas said. "I lost it. Sometimes that's all you can do."

Chapter Nineteen

When he climbed out of bed the next morning, his throat still throbbed, which was the only way he knew he hadn't dreamed up everything that had happened. Thomas did a quick wash and comb, appraising the damage to his neck. It was bruised and swollen, and he wrapped a wool scarf around it before heading up.

On deck, the bright light of the sun stung his eyes. He felt woozy and off balance. He stood gripping the railing, hoping to come back to himself somehow. He was still not feeling much better when Priska ran up to him.

"What happened? There are all these stories going around . . . an accident . . . did Holz really go overboard?"

Thomas nodded. He preferred to talk as little as he could, given the pain in his throat.

Priska brought her hand to her mouth. "Are you all right?"

"Yes."

She seemed to know that there was more to the story and that he would tell her everything in time. That she needn't rush him.

"Just tell me one thing: Were you right about the money?"

He shook his head. "They were plans. Blueprints of U.S. planes. I threw them overboard. Priska, he was a Nazi spy."

She smiled. "I can't believe it. And you got rid of the plans? You're a hero! And, Thomas, we're not going back to Germany! France, Belgium, Holland, and England have agreed to take us. Every last one of us on board. The Joint brokered a resolution. We've been saved!"

Thomas was still too dazed to really comprehend the news. He tried to understand it all—he would not be re-united with Walter, but if he was lucky, he would find a new life somewhere else. He thought about how Priska had said he could live with them. Maybe he would, after all.

For the remainder of the voyage, the ship came back to life. There was dancing, singing, joking. They played the usual deck games and even had a giant game of tug-of-war. Thirty-five days after they had left Hamburg, they docked in Antwerp. The representative from the Joint who had brokered the resolution came aboard to help decide which countries the passengers would go to.

Thomas and Priska went to the social hall and stood outside the closed doors, looking in through the window. Soon Paul and Claudia came out. "I did the best I could," Paul was saying to her.

"How's it going in there?" Priska asked as she chewed on a fingernail.

"Nine hundred people is a lot to sort out," Paul replied.

"Where do you hope to go?" Priska asked.

"I have relatives in France," Claudia said.

Priska looked at Thomas. "We don't care where we go as long as Thomas is with us."

Claudia assured her, "They said families would remain together."

"Your father will try his best," Thomas said.

"The countries are fighting over the people with the most favorable U.S. quota numbers," Paul explained. "That way they won't be a burden on that country very long because they'll soon be going to America."

Thomas and Priska walked back out to the deck. Günther, Ingrid, Marianne, Jakob, and Hannelore were huddled together.

"Any news yet?" Günther asked.

Thomas shook his head.

Ingrid suggested they play shuffleboard to pass the time, but no one wanted to. Finally, around five p.m., a voice came over the loudspeaker: "The passengers who will disembark in Antwerp in preparation for transfer to elsewhere in Belgium and Holland have been decided. If your name is one of those called, please go to the dining rooms to have a light dinner. You will be disembarking in two hours' time."

Thomas froze, listening intently to the names as they were called. He told himself not to get his hopes up. Most likely he would not be with her. But then he heard Priska's voice in his head, telling him to have faith.

"Blanka Rosen, Siegfried Adler, Pauline Einhorn . . . Emil Affeldt, Flora Affeldt, Priska Affeldt, Marianne Affeldt . . ."

Thomas glanced at Priska.

Marianne said, "What about Thomas?"

"Shh," Priska warned, holding a hand up to silence both of them.

Thomas stood still, numb all over. With each name, his hope diminished. When the list was finished, his name had not been called.

"We're leaving," Priska said, her face blank.

Marianne burst into tears and ran to Thomas. He wrapped his arms around her. "We'll see each other again soon. This is just for the time being. We'll meet in America." Thomas couldn't believe the words coming from his mouth—promises he couldn't guarantee. He met Priska's eyes over Marianne's head. She mouthed his name.

Thomas patted Marianne on the back. "Your father will be looking for you two. You need to have dinner. You can't travel on an empty stomach."

"I'm not hungry," Marianne said.

He forced a smile. "You? Not hungry? That will be the day!"

On the way to the dining hall, Priska walked close to Thomas. He smiled at her. He was holding it together for her and for Marianne too.

"There you are," Professor Affeldt said, walking toward them. He looked from Priska to Thomas. "I'm sorry. I tried."

"I understand," Thomas said.

"Did you try everything, Vati?" Priska asked. "You said he was our cousin?"

"Yes, of course, but, darling, you don't know how lucky we are that these countries have agreed to take us in the first place." He reached out to her but she turned away from him. Professor Affeldt continued, "No one is going back to Germany. They've assured us of that." He sighed and then said, "We should go eat."

Priska looked at Thomas. "I want to spend this last hour with you."

"Of course he'll join us," Professor Affeldt said.

"No," she said, still facing Thomas. "I want to be on deck with you. I want to be alone with you." Thomas couldn't help but notice how Priska's alliances seemed to have shifted.

"All right," Professor Affeldt said. "I'll see if I can take something to bring with us in case you get hungry later."

Priska took Thomas's hand and they walked to the railing overlooking the quayside. Below, deck boys carried luggage down the gangway.

"I can't believe I'm getting off," Priska said. "It felt as if we'd be on this ship forever, and now in a matter of hours it's all over. I know I should be happy, but where will you be sent? How will I know? How will we find each other again?"

Thomas heard a strange calmness in his own voice as he answered, "We'll write to each other once we're settled."

Priska's voice was near panic. "But how will I know where you are? And who knows where we're going exactly?"

"We just have to trust that somehow we'll find each other again." Thomas raised his eyebrows and smiled. "We have to have faith."

"Don't make fun of me," she said.

"I'm not making fun of you. Not really."

Priska looked at the dock. "I know, let's make a pact—"

Thomas furrowed his brow.

"If for some reason we don't find each other, in five years' time we'll meet. On this very day in five years. June 17, 1944. This craziness will surely be long over by then. I'll be nineteen and you'll be twenty."

Thomas tried to imagine himself at twenty but couldn't. He couldn't even imagine what he'd be like an hour after Priska had left the ship.

"We'll meet in Miami," Priska continued. "We'll both be in America by then. We'll meet by the harbor where the ships come in. Where we would have docked."

Thomas stared at her, trying to carve her features into his mind.

"All right?" She extended her hand to shake on it. Her eyes were wide open and he knew he would surprise her, but he wasn't passing up his last chance. Thomas leaned in and touched his lips to hers. They stood together, lips pressed against lips, joining themselves, until Paul and Claudia walked by.

"Young love," Claudia said to Paul.

Priska pulled away and giggled.

"Five years from this very day," Thomas repeated. "If we don't find each other before then."

—∞—

Franz, Claudia, and Paul were among the passengers disembarking in Antwerp. Franz shook Thomas's hand.

"If you ever get to America, make sure you see Lasker play."

"I will," Thomas said. "Good luck."

Next, Thomas shook hands with Professor Affeldt, hugged Marianne, and held Priska against him. Almost everyone assigned to Antwerp had filed off.

"Priska, we need to go," Professor Affeldt called. "Thomas, take care."

Priska moved away but held on to Thomas's hand. She let her hand slip from his until they were just touching fingertips. Then they were no longer touching at all.

Thomas watched Priska walk down the gangway, feeling as if the air around him were disappearing with her. His throat, still sore, was closing up. Just before the end of the gangway, she turned and waved. She was smiling her wide smile, and all of a sudden he could breathe again.

Five years. Miami. If not before.

Ten Years After the Voyage

Thomas stood on the pier in Miami, looking out over the water. It was blazing hot out and he wiped away a trickle of sweat from his forehead. They should have picked a time of day. Not just a day, but a time of day. But they had been so young, and with all that had been going on around them, he could understand why they hadn't been more specific. And anyway, they had planned to meet five years after, and now it was ten. He hadn't been able to come five years after, or the next year either. They had been so naive to think everything would be back to normal by 1944. In '44 the war was still going, and nothing would ever be back to normal again for those who lived through it.

He had come every year since '46, but she had never shown up, and he had told himself that this was the last time he would come. If she didn't come today, well, then he would know what had happened to her.

He rubbed the toe of his shoe against the grain of the wood of the pier. He looked out at the ships dotting the harbor. No liners today. In '47 he'd been at this very spot when the liners were boarding. How strange it had been to see the people getting on. Even now it was still hard to reconcile being on this side instead of out there, floating.

The day grew hotter as the sun bore down on him, but he would wait all day if he had to. He wouldn't leave. Not until the sun had set, officially ending the day and his last remaining hopes.

He hadn't worn a watch, but from the sun's position in the sky he guessed it was near three o'clock when he noticed a woman coming down the pier. As she came closer, he saw she had curly hair that bounced against her shoulders. Seeing him, she broke into a jog and then pulled up fif-. teen feet away from him. He wondered if he looked that different. He carried himself differently, he knew that much. He felt more confident in his own body, but one shoulder sloped downward in a strange way, on account of a gunshot wound. It was fully functional, just looked a little odd.

"Thomas?"

His heart felt as if it would soar right out of his chest. She was here. They had found each other. She was alive. He stepped toward her, squinting. He had thought about this moment time and time again, only now something wasn't right. Well, of course, the war had changed her. It had changed them all. Who knew what she had lived through?

She must have seen his confusion because she took a sharp inward breath and said, "No. No, it's Marianne. I'm sorry." She had started crying. Tears pouring down her face. He knew those tears. They were the same ones he had inside him. They stayed buried until they surged forth uncontrollably. "Priska told me she had promised to meet you."

Thomas looked away. "She didn't make it."

"She died in Auschwitz." Marianne paused, as if she was still trying to get used to saying those words. She continued, "I didn't know if you had survived. I hoped so much you had. I wanted you to know. I tried to find you, but I couldn't find record of any Thomas Werkmann from Berlin. I needed to find you and tell you, and now I have." She smiled, tears still wet on her face. "You're alive."

"Yes," he said, and he felt it painfully—his being alive, and Priska not.

Marianne brushed away her tears. After a while Thomas broke the silence. "Do you know what happened to some of the others? Günther, Ingrid, Jakob . . ."

"I don't know. I ran into Paul at the camp for displaced persons that I was sent to after the war. He said Claudia was killed."

Thomas closed his eyes briefly. "We thought we were saved. . . ."

"Yes, we all did. How were we to know that the war would soon start and the Nazis would be invading France and Holland?"

Thomas sighed. "What happened to your family after you left the ship?"

"We first went into a quarantine camp, and then we were transferred to the Lloyd Hotel in Amsterdam, where we shared an apartment with another family. We actually went to school—a Jewish school in Amsterdam. Life was all right in a way. Then the occupation came." Marianne glanced away from Thomas. "Mutti wanted us to go into hiding, but that meant we'd likely have to split up and Vati didn't want to do that. Before we could decide, we were taken to the Westerbork internment camp on the German border. Again, at the beginning it wasn't so bad. But by 1942, the Germans took over the camp and everything changed. We had to work in the fields all day, and more people were crammed into our small room. Then they started taking people away on the transports. Every Tuesday a train would leave. My father was the first to go. About four months later my mother, Priska, and I were sent to Auschwitz. When we got off the train, they made two lines. My mother went to the left and we went to the right. We never saw her or my father again. Priska died of typhoid a few weeks before the camp was liberated."

Marianne breathed deeply. Thomas watched her chest rise and fall. She was skinny and he remembered her voracious appetite.

She asked, "Where were you sent? We never knew."

"I was lucky," he said. "I was sent to England. In England we were classified as enemy aliens because we were German." Thomas shook his head at the irony of it all—

that he, a Jew, could somehow be an enemy of the forces opposed to Hitler.

"I went on to volunteer for the Alien Companies of the Pioneer Corps. I fought against the Nazis in France in 1940. Later I was transferred to an elite commando division. We parachuted behind enemy lines to do reconnaissance in advance of British units. That's when my name changed from Werkmann to Workman. That's probably why you couldn't find me. They wanted us to be British, not German, and that was fine with me. All my time fighting for the Allied forces, I was relatively happy. All I ever wanted was to fight the Nazis, in whichever way I could."

Marianne nodded. "Yes, you always were so courageous."

"Really?" It was odd to think that was how she had thought of him. He remembered then that she'd fancied him. He flushed a bit to think of it, even now. He continued, "After the war I came here. My brother was already here by then. My mother came too. My father died in Dachau."

Thomas saw what looked like a ghost of the moon high in the sky. It never made sense to him why sometimes you could see the moon in the plain light of day.

"Do you still have your good appetite?"

She chuckled. "Yes."

"Will you have dinner with me?"

"That would be nice."

Seventy Years After the Voyage

Standing outside the museum, Thomas had a change of heart. He wanted to turn around and forget the whole thing. But next to him was Marianne, and next to her were their son and daughter, Seth and Faith. And they had all made the trip to D.C. from New York. Certainly all three might have understood if he said he couldn't go through with it—Marianne, in particular. But he had never agreed to do something and then not done it, and now was no time to start.

The museum was quieter than any other he'd ever been in. It was as if it had been built on the foundation of those eleven million lost souls. Once he set foot in the Hall of Witness, he had to stop and remind his old lungs to breathe. The brick walls felt as if they were closing in on him. He looked up at the giant skylight and felt dizzy. Again, he thought of turning back, of scrapping the whole visit, but he took a deep breath and headed toward the wide staircase that led to the exhibits. There was so much to see at the museum, but at his age he had to conserve energy. They would go first to the exhibit on the *St. Francis.* If there was time and strength left, they could explore more afterward.

At the sign that pointed the way to the exhibit, Marianne took his hand, squeezed it, and then released it as if she was telling him she was there if he needed her.

"Ready?"

He nodded, his throat already thick with memories.

He moved from one oversized photograph to the next. Seth's and Faith's eyes were wide. They knew little of the story beyond that he and Marianne had been on the ship the whole world had turned its back on. For so many years he had wanted nothing to do with any of those memories. *The past should stay in the past,* he had always said as an excuse not to tell them much about his own childhood in Berlin or his life during the war. Perhaps Marianne had told them more—he wasn't sure.

There was text alongside the images but he didn't need the narrative—this story was his. Names and faces of passengers that he hadn't thought of in years flooded back to him: Frau Rosen, Herr Kleist, Franz, Wilhelm. He recognized some of those very people in the photographs.

Thomas paused at a picture of the captain. Thomas had kept up with what had happened to him more than he had with anyone else on board. The trip to Cuba hadn't been his last voyage after all. Later that year he had helmed the *St. Francis* on its usual summer-holiday voyages from Germany to the Caribbean. When war had broken out that September, the ship had been on its way to Bermuda and he had managed to bring it safely back to Hamburg. It was his final voyage; the captain never returned to sea. He took a desk job during the war, and afterward he was put on trial for collaborating with the Nazis. Thomas and other surviving passengers of the *St. Francis* had written a letter testifying on his behalf. Thomas had found out that the captain had indeed been the main reason they were treated so well on board and served the best meals. The shipping line had wanted to cut costs by lowering the standards, but he had insisted on nothing less than the best. The captain was acquitted and later recognized for his efforts to help the passengers of the *St. Francis* to safety.

As for Manfred, Thomas often thought about him and wondered what had happened to him. He would likely never know.

Thomas moved to the next photograph and his breath caught in his throat. When Marianne had told him she was planning to donate their photographs to the United States Holocaust Memorial Museum, he had agreed it was a good idea. He had looked at them quickly before she sent them off, but now here they were, blown up to almost life-size. He and Günther halfway up the mast. Priska, Ingrid, and Marianne in a lifeboat. He stopped short before the next photograph.

There she was: front and center. Her curly hair, her wide eyes, her mischievous smile. All of them were grouped around the life ring with the words ST. FRANCIS emblazoned on it, but he saw only her. While he had forgotten many of those other people who had been on board the *St. Francis,* not a day had passed that he hadn't thought of her. On his wedding day, on the days when his children and grandchildren had been born—he thought of her then too.

"Doesn't she look beautiful," Marianne said.

"That's your sister?" Seth asked.

Marianne nodded.

"That's who my Priska is named after," Faith said of her own young daughter, who had stayed at home in New York with Faith's husband.

Thomas wondered if Seth or Faith could tell from the photograph how he had loved Priska. He was standing close to her, and the lens had caught him looking at her, not at the camera. It was certainly no secret to Marianne that he had loved her and always would. They had discussed as much before he asked her to marry him. In fact, he shared with Marianne that love for Priska. It was one of the many things that bound them together.

"It says here the United States decided not to let you in," Faith said.

"They should have," Marianne replied. "If anything, they could have taken us temporarily."

Faith pointed to a reproduction of a page from the *New York Times*. "You were front-page news."

"We didn't know that back then, of course," Thomas said. "We were in our own little bubble on the ship, and what news reached us couldn't always be trusted either."

"Why didn't the United States let you in?" Seth said.

Thomas clucked. "They had quota numbers and procedures to follow. We appealed to Roosevelt. Priska even wrote a letter to Eleanor Roosevelt—we never got a response from her, but later I did hear she had tried to help us."

Faith shook her head. She had what Thomas liked to think of as the Affeldt family curls. "They should have made an exception. It's like how the United States could have bombed the rail lines to Auschwitz once they knew what was happening there, but they didn't."

"It would have saved a lot of lives," Marianne agreed. "Over seven hundred of us had quota numbers for the U.S. already—it just would have meant taking us a little early."

"You didn't hold a grudge?" Seth asked.

Thomas shrugged. "Things got too complicated for grudges. Your uncle Walter was here . . . so much had happened."

Thomas read a few lines of the text underneath a photograph of the *St. Francis* docking in Antwerp. The passengers looked tired but happy. Thomas remembered how they had all thought they were saved. "Two hundred fifty-four of us on the ship ended up dying in the Holocaust?" he read out loud. "Did you know it was that many, Marianne?" He sorted through the names he remembered: Günther, Ingrid, Hannelore, Franz, Wilhelm, Jürgen, Frau Rosen. Many of them had certainly been killed.

Marianne shook her head. "We were the lucky ones."

Before they left the exhibit, Thomas went back to the photograph of them all huddled around the life ring. He reached out and touched her face with his fingers, hoping to feel something besides the glass that encased the photograph. But all he was left with was an impression of cold.

He wouldn't remember seeing other parts of the museum. He walked numbly through the corridors, not even feeling the age of his body. He didn't realize Marianne was holding his hand until they exited the museum. The sun was bright and he went to shield his eyes, only to find his hand attached to hers.

"Are you okay?"

"Mmm," he replied. He staggered a bit as he walked, off-kilter from the sun's glare and from the memories, which reverberated over seventy years. Being unsteady on his feet reminded him of the day rough seas had hit the ship and so many had been seasick. The memories would stay with him. They were what he had left of her.

Chronology of Selected Anti-Semitic Acts and Actions of the Third Reich

March 1933
Dachau, the first concentration camp, was established for "enemies of the state."

April 1933
Jews were no longer allowed to be teachers, professors, or judges unless they had fought on the front line during World War I.

German schools reduced their number of Jewish students.

October 1933
Jews were forced to give up jobs as editors of newspapers.

May 1935
Jews were no longer allowed to serve in the German army.

September 1935
Jews lost their status as German citizens, which meant that they could not vote or hold public office.

It became a crime for German citizens to marry Jews. Sexual relations outside marriage between German citizens and Jews also were deemed a crime.

Jews could not employ Germans as household helpers, such as cleaners or cooks.

Jews were not allowed to hang the Reich flag or the German flag at their homes.

December 1935
Jewish soldiers who had died serving Germany in World War I could no longer be honored on war memorials.

January 1936
Jews who worked as tax consultants had to give up their jobs.

April 1936
Jews who worked as veterinarians were forced to give up their jobs.

October 1936
Jews were banned from teaching in public schools.

January 1937
The Reich discouraged Germans from seeking medical attention from Jewish doctors.

April 1937
Berlin public schools closed their doors to Jewish children.

January 1938
Jews were no longer allowed to change their names.

April 1938
Jews were similarly forbidden to change the names of Jewish-owned businesses.

It became compulsory for Jews to report any property valued at 5,000 reichsmarks or more.

July 1938
Jews were no longer allowed in health spas.

September 1938
Jews lost the right to practice law.

October 1938
The Reich decreed that all German passports held by Jews would be invalid unless stamped with a "J."

November 1938
The Reich shuttered all Jewish businesses.

The Reich prohibited Jewish children from attending public schools.

Jews were no longer allowed in cinemas, theaters, or sports facilities.

November 9–10, 1938

In an organized action called *Reichskristallnacht,* or the "night of broken glass," Nazis destroyed synagogues, shops, and homes, killed more than ninety Jews, and arrested over twenty thousand of them, sending them to concentration camps.

February 1939

Jews were ordered to give the Reich all their gold and silver, with the exception of wedding rings.

Chronology is based partly on information from the United States Holocaust Memorial Museum: "Examples of Antisemitic Legislation, 1933–1939," *Holocaust Encyclopedia* (www.ushmm.org/wlc/article.php?lang= en&ModuleId=10007459, accessed October 17, 2008).

More information about anti-Semitic legislation and actions can be found at the United States Holocaust Memorial Museum Web site: www.ushmm.org.

Author's Note

*T*he *Other Half of Life* is based on the true story of the MS ("motor ship") *St. Louis,* which left Hamburg, Germany, on May 13, 1939, bound for Havana, Cuba. It carried 937 passengers, the majority of whom were Jews escaping Nazi Germany.

Among the people I spoke to during my research was a man who fled Germany with his family in 1938. He explained that someone who had not lived through his experiences could never understand or truly convey the mind-set of the period, which is so foreign to the climate of freedom we enjoy in America today. This is probably correct, but I still felt that bringing the voyage of the *St. Louis* back to life for a new generation was a worthy task.

What in *The Other Half of Life* is accurate and what is fiction? When it was possible, I stayed true to the events and timetable of the voyage. But there is plenty in these pages that I imagined or altered to fit my story.

The following are all true:

There were young people traveling alone aboard the ship, as well as a crew member who was hiding his Jewish identity. The captain was indeed a principled and ethical man who insisted on treating his Jewish passengers like anyone else. And there was a German underground group opposed to Hitler whose mission was to compile information on anti-Nazi sentiment and make it known to other countries. A Nazi spy from the *Abwehr*—the German intelligence organization—was aboard the ship, and he picked up secret papers in Havana and carried them back to Germany. While no one knows what the papers were, there is speculation that they held information on American military equipment.

Ultimately, the ship was turned away by Cuba and other Latin American countries, Canada, and the United States of America. After much negotiation, France, Holland, Belgium, and Great Britain agreed to take the passengers. Tragically, 254 of the 937 people on board the *St. Louis* perished in the Holocaust.[1] Many of the surviving passengers eventually immigrated to the United States.

The *St. Louis* left an indelible legacy in helping to shape our country's humanitarian treatment of refugees, and influenced legislation such as the 1948 Displaced Persons Act and the 1980 Refugee Act. Because of the United States' history as a safe haven for people seeking freedom, it continues to struggle with the complex and controversial issue of how many refugees to admit.

---

[1] Bloomfield, Sara J., foreword to *Refuge Denied: The* St. Louis *Passengers and the Holocaust* (Madison: University of Wisconsin Press, 2006), p. x.

Acknowledgments

I would like to acknowledge the following people who helped me throughout my research and writing:

I owe a great debt of gratitude to Herbert Karliner for sharing the story of his family's journey aboard the *St. Louis* and his life afterward. Mr. Karliner also was kind enough to read the manuscript, and it means so very much to me that he was happy with it. Thank you also to Ed Goldstein for talking to me about prewar Jewish life and how his family decided to leave Germany; Lamelle Ryman for her expertise on Judaism; Luke Evans Calhoun of the Harvard University Chess Club for his amazing guidance in all chess matters; Professor Murray Schwartz of Emerson College for his vast knowledge of World War II and the Holocaust; Jack Putnam of the South Street Seaport Museum, which houses the collection from the Ocean Liner Museum; the Newton Free Library, where most of this book was researched and written; and the United States Holocaust Memorial Museum. Thanks, too, to Rose Brock, librarian at Coppell Middle School West, Coppell, Texas, and Kenneth Kugler, young adult librarian at Queens Library, Jamaica, New York, for reviewing the manuscript. I would also like to thank my

Acknowledgments

agent, Jeff Dwyer; my wonderful editor, Nancy Hinkel, who encouraged me to write this book; and the many other integral people at Knopf, including Allison Wortche, Jenny Golub, Artie Bennett, Barbara Perris, Alison Kolani, and Kate Gartner. My writing friends helped me every step of the way: Cara Crandall, Lynne Heitman, Mike Wiecek, and Samantha Cameron. Finally, on a personal note, I couldn't have written this without the support of Matt, my mom and my dad, Mary Flaherty, and Maggie O'Brien, who all made it possible for me to find time to write.

Selected Sources on the MS St. Louis

Books

Morse, Arthur D. *While Six Million Died: A Chronicle of American Apathy.* Woodstock, NY: The Overlook Press, 1983.

Ogilvie, Sarah A., and Scott Miller. *Refuge Denied: The* St. Louis *Passengers and the Holocaust.* Madison: University of Wisconsin Press, 2006.

Thomas, Gordon, and Max Morgan Witts. *Voyage of the Damned.* Mattituck, NY: Amereon House, 1974.

Videos & DVDs

The Double Crossing: The Voyage of the St. Louis. Holocaust Memorial Foundation of Illinois and Loyola University, Chicago. Distributed by Ergo Media, Inc., Teaneck, NJ, 1992.

Sea Tales: The Doomed Voyage of the St. Louis. Distributed by A&E Home Entertainment, New York, 1996.

Online Sources

United States Holocaust Memorial Museum Online. "Voyage of the St. Louis," www.ushmm.org/museum/exhibit/online/stlouis (October 17, 2008).

Sources on the Holocaust

Edelheit, Abraham J., and Hershel Edelheit. *History of the Holocaust: A Handbook and Dictionary*. Boulder, CO: Westview Press, 1994.

Edelheit, Hershel, and Abraham J. Edelheit. *A World in Turmoil: An Integrated Chronology of the Holocaust and World War II*. Westport, CT: Greenwood Press, 1991.

Evans, Richard J. *The Third Reich in Power*. New York: The Penguin Press, 2005.

Schoeps, Karl-Heinz. *Literature and Film in the Third Reich*. Translated by Kathleen M. Dell'Orto. Suffolk, England: Boydell & Brewer, 2004.

Sources on German Resistance

Benz, Wolfgang, and Walter H. Pehle. *Encyclopedia of German Resistance to the Nazi Movement*. Translated by Lance W. Garmer. New York: The Continuum Publishing Company, 1997.

Gill, Anton. *An Honourable Defeat: A History of German Resistance to Hitler, 1933–1945*. New York: Henry Holt, 1994.

Hoffmann, Peter. *The History of the German Resistance, 1933–1945*. Translated by Richard Barry. Cambridge, MA: MIT Press, 1977.

Peukert, Detlev J. K. *Inside Nazi Germany: Conformity, Opposition, and Racism in Everyday Life*. Translated by Richard Deveson. New Haven, CT: Yale University Press, 1987.

Thomsett, Michael C. *The German Opposition to Hitler: The Resistance, the Underground, and Assassination Plots, 1938–1945*. Jefferson, NC: McFarland & Co., 1997.

Von Klemperer, Klemens. *German Resistance Against Hitler: The Search for Allies Abroad, 1938–1945*. New York: Oxford University Press, 1993.

Sources on Ocean Liners

Hansen, Clas Broder. *Passenger Liners from Germany, 1816–1990*. Translated by Dr. Edward Force. West Chester, PA: Schiffer Publishing, 1991.

Hunter-Cox, Jane. *Ocean Pictures: The Golden Age of Transatlantic Travel, 1936 to 1959*. London: Webb & Bower, 1989.

Maddocks, Melvin. *The Great Liners*. Alexandria, VA: Time Life Books, 1978.

Maxtone-Graham, John. *Crossing & Cruising: From the Golden Era of Ocean Liners to the Luxury Cruise Ships of Today*. New York: Scribner, 1992.

Maxtone-Graham, John. *The Only Way to Cross*. New York: Macmillan, 1972.

McAuley, Rob. *The Liners: A Voyage of Discovery*. Osceola, WI: Motorbooks International, 1997.

Miller, William H., Jr. *The Great Luxury Liners, 1927–1954: A Photographic Record*. New York: Dover Publications, 1981.

Sources on Chess

Gelo, James H. *Chess World Championships: All the Games, All with Diagrams, 1834–2004*. Jefferson, NC: McFarland & Co., 2006.

Hannak, J. *Emanuel Lasker: The Life of a Chess Master*. New York: Simon & Schuster, 1959.

Lasker, Emanuel. *Lasker's Manual of Chess*. New York: Dover Publications, 1947.

Questions for Discussion

1. As Thomas works his way through the ship to the upper deck, he listens to people talk about what they used to have—homes, possessions, businesses, professions. He wonders why people insist on clinging to memories that only seem to bring pain. Do the Jews' memories of what they have lost only bring them pain? Why or why not?

2. Though attracted to each other, Thomas and Priska have differences that seem to make it impossible for them to be together. What are these differences? How do Thomas and Priska finally overcome them?

3. The captain is a good man and insists on equal treatment for his Jewish passengers. What problems does this create? How does the captain maintain control of the Nazi officers on the ship?

4. One of the lessons Thomas learned from his father was to trust his intuition. How does this lesson prove to be valuable in light of what Thomas and Priska discover about the Ortsgruppenleiter? Does their discovery help the passengers?

5. What is the basis for the competition between Manfred and Thomas? How do they try to prove who is the better man? Why does Manfred have the upper hand? Why does Manfred save Thomas from Kurt instead of beating him up?

6. Thomas has a difficult time restraining himself from talking back to the Nazis on the ship, which causes trouble for him and the older Jewish men who try to keep him in line. Thomas finally begins to understand what his father taught him: "We need to live to fight, not fight to live" (p. 121). What might this mean to a Jew in 1939? Does the meaning change for our society today?

7. Thomas knows little about the Jewish religion, but he learns a great deal from Priska and her family. He feels at peace when he attends Shabbat, but he does not understand the rabbi's words: "More than the people of Israel have kept Shabbos, Shabbos has kept the people of Israel" (p. 109). What does the rabbi mean by this statement?

8. Even though Priska's family has status, and they travel first-class, they are discontent and face problems. How does Priska's family compare to Thomas's? What impact have their families had on each of their characters?

9. Why is a chess tournament a good way to keep the passengers occupied while they wait for news of disembarking? What events occur during the tournament that could prove to be disastrous? What does Thomas learn about Manfred that gives him insight into Manfred's actions?

10. Why do the officials in so many countries refuse sanctuary for the Jews aboard the MS *St. Francis*? Would the officials have refused if they had known they were sending the passengers to their death?

Prepared by Susan Geye, Library Media Specialist, Fort Worth, Texas